PUFFIN BOOKS

SHARK ADVENTURE

Anthony McGowan is a multi-award-winning author of books for adults, teenagers and younger children. He has a life-long obsession with the natural world, and has travelled widely to study and observe it.

Books by Anthony McGowan

LEOPARD ADVENTURE

SHARK ADVENTURE

SHARK ADVENTURE

ANTHONY McGOWAN

Illustrated by David Shephard

Set in Baskerville MT Std 13/19pt by Palimpsest Book Production Ltd, Falkirk,
Printed in Great Britain by Clays Ltd, St Ives plc

This book is sold subject to the condition that it shall not, by way of trade or otherwise, be lent, resold, hired out, or otherwise circulated without the publisher's prior consent in any form of binding or cover other than that in which it is published and without a similar condition including this condition being imposed on the subsequent purchaser

British Library Cataloguing in Publication Data
A CIP catalogue record for this book is available from the British Library

PUFFIN

PUFFIN BOOKS

Published by the Penguin Group
Penguin Books Ltd, 80 Strand, London WC2R ORL, England
Penguin Group (USA) Inc., 375 Hudson Street, New York, New York 10014, USA
Penguin Group (Canada), 90 Eglinton Avenue East, Suite 700, Toronto, Ontario, Canada M4P 2Y3
(a division of Pearson Penguin Canada Inc.)
Penguin Ireland, 25 St Stephen's Green, Dublin 2, Ireland (a division of Penguin Books Ltd)
Penguin Group (Australia), 707 Collins Street, Melbourne, Victoria 3008, Australia
(a division of Pearson Australia Group Pty Ltd)
Penguin Books India Pvt Ltd, 11 Community Centre, Panchsheel Park, New Delhi – 110 017, India
Penguin Group (NZ), 67 Apollo Drive, Rosedale, Auckland 0632, New Zealand
(a division of Pearson New Zealand Ltd)
Penguin Books (South Africa) (Pty) Ltd, Block D, Rosebank Office Park, 181 Jan Smuts Avenue, Parktown
North, Gauteng 2193, South Africa

Penguin Books Ltd, Registered Offices: 80 Strand, London WC2R ORL, England

puffinbooks.com

First published 2013
001

Text and illustrations copyright © Helena Pierce Anderson [...], 2013
Map copyright © [...]

Se[...] Stirlingshire
Printed in [...]

British Library Cataloguing in Publication Data
A catalogue record for this book is available from the British Library

ISBN: 978-0-141-33948-1

www.greenpenguin.co.uk

ALWAYS LEARNING   **PEARSON**

To the wonderful people and astonishing wildlife of the remote islands of Polynesia

Contents

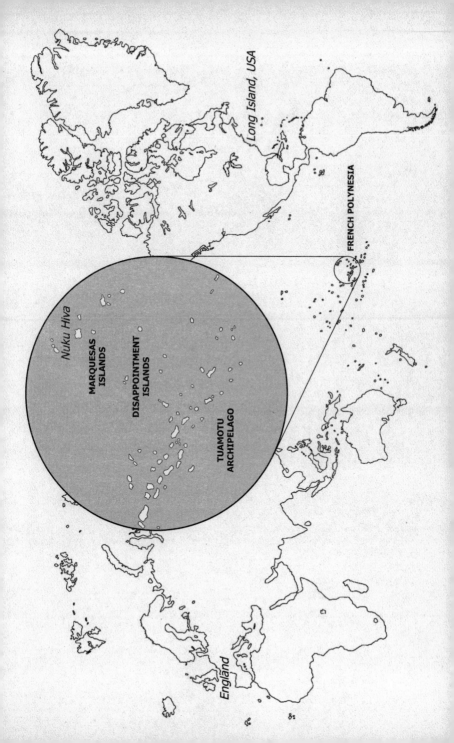

The Turtle's Story

Her ancestors had been doing this for a hundred million years: returning to the same isolated beaches to lay their eggs. Those ancestors had shared the ancient seas with long-necked plesiosaurs, fast-swimming ichthyosaurs and the terrifying mosasaurs, built like monumental crocodiles, with jaws capable of engulfing a fully grown leatherback turtle, whole.

She herself had made this journey a hundred times. Now she was tired. So tired. She would not come to this beach – or any other – ever again. And the knowledge that this was her last time gave extra urgency to the long, slow beating of her flippers.

She found the familiar gap in the reef and entered the calm lagoon. She surfaced and saw above her the great canopy of stars, like frozen fireworks. Soon she felt the sand on the underside of her shell, and began to drag herself up the beach. So graceful in the water, on land she was ungainly and awkward, moving as if carrying a great burden, and it was not long before she reached a point beyond exhaustion.

But she had to make it past the high-tide mark or her eggs would be swamped and lost; and so on she went. At last she found a place where the white coral sand was untouched by the waves, and she began to dig, pushing down with her back flippers and flicking the sand out in all directions, like a garden sprinkler.

It took her almost an hour, but finally she was content with the depth of the hole, and she began to lay. It took her another hour to fill her nest with the hundred and fifty eggs. When it was over, she pushed back the sand. It was still dark, but there was a slight lightening in the east as she hauled herself back to the warm sea.

The ache in her stomach told her that she hadn't eaten for a long time, and she thought it would be good to swim through a swarm of jellyfish, munching away. Their stings couldn't hurt her, and the soft bodies were easy on her old jaws. She moved serenely through the gap in the reef, her front flippers beating the water like leathery wings, and she sensed the bottom fall away to the dark, cold depths.

And then she felt something else. A movement, dark against the dark. Something huge, and deadly, and without pity.

She had fought sharks before. She knew where they were vulnerable. Her sharp, hooked beak could inflict serious damage on a shark's gills. And her sheer bulk – she was two metres long and weighed more than 700 kg – made her a surprisingly formidable foe. And, besides, she was too tired to run. So she took a last gulp of air, and thinking perhaps of the tens of thousands of eggs she had laid, of the many thousands of young who had struggled down to the water, of the few who had made it through to adulthood, she dived to face the shadow as it rose.

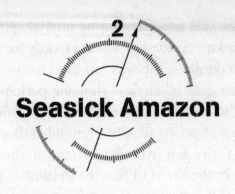

2

Seasick Amazon

Amazon Hunt was dying. Absolutely, definitely dying. There was a savage beast trying to burst out of her skull, and she writhed and twisted as if electric currents were being passed through her body. She was consumed by nausea so intense that even her fingertips felt sick. The wooden walls surrounding her heaved and moved like they were alive. She was convinced that those walls hated her, and she hated them back.

In her hand she clutched her most prized possession: the red neckerchief with white spots given to her by her mother years earlier, before Amazon was sent to boarding school. It gave her some comfort. But not enough.

'I'm dying,' she moaned through dry, cracked lips.

'You're not dying,' sighed her cousin, Frazer Hunt, for the hundredth time.

'I am *so* dying. Pass me the sick bucket.'

'You don't need the sick bucket,' said Frazer, as patiently as he could. He might also have added that

4

the sick bucket was full, but he tactfully refrained. 'What you need is some fresh air. Come on, I'll help you up on deck.'

'It'll be like a holiday,' Amazon's Uncle Hal had said, as they waited in the departure lounge at Vancouver Airport.

They were in Canada to search for Amazon's mother and father, whose light aircraft had gone missing in highly suspicious circumstances somewhere in the wilderness.

'I don't want a holiday. I want to help you find my mum and dad,' Amazon had pleaded.

But Hal Hunt's logic had been remorseless, and a little brutal.

'I understand that, Amazon,' he had said. 'But, frankly, you're more of a hindrance than a help – you are only thirteen, remember. We would have to divert resources to take care of you. Resources that could be better employed on the search.'

Hal Hunt, his grizzled hair cut short, military style, wasn't someone you argued with. He was the undisputed head of TRACKS – the Trans-Regional Animal Conservation and Knowledge Society – and he was used to getting his way. Despite being almost sixty years old, he still gave off an aura of strength and determination.

But Amazon knew that there was a core of kindness underneath his hard exterior.

'Besides, after what you've been through in Siberia these last few weeks, you've earned a place on another TRACKS mission,' he added.

Amazon had learned a lot about both herself and the wide world in the few weeks since she had been whisked from Millbank Abbey, her pretty but dull boarding school in the English countryside, and taken to the TRACKS HQ on Long Island in the United States.

The plan had been to meet her parents, Ling-Mei and Roger, there. This was a miracle in its own right. The brothers Hal and Roger Hunt had not spoken for many years. Although they were both dedicated to saving animals and preserving the natural world, and had set up TRACKS together, they differed over the direction that the organization should take. Hal wanted to expand its reach and power by taking on corporate sponsorship and funding from governments; Roger preferred to keep the operation small and flexible and, crucially, independent.

Hal won the argument, and so TRACKS had developed into a well-resourced and powerful organization, able to send teams of young environmentalists – the Trackers – around the world on emergency projects and longer conservation programmes.

The split became a family feud that had lasted long enough for Amazon never to have met her cousin Frazer, Hal's son. That all changed the day he helped her climb in through her dormitory window at Millbank and brought her back to the TRACKS HQ in America.

Her parents were supposed to have some vitally important information about TRACKS. It was information they had not been able to impart, for, when Amazon reached Long Island, she found out that her parents' light aircraft had gone missing in the west of Canada, and Hal Hunt was leading a rescue mission to find them.

Partly to keep Amazon's mind off this, she and Frazer went on an expedition to help save one of the world's rarest big cats – the Amur leopard – in the remote forests of Siberia. It was a mission that led them all into incredible danger at the hands of poachers, and at the claws of a fearsome Siberian tiger.

'This is going to be so cool!' chipped in Frazer. 'I've always wanted to go to a South Sea island. Think of it, Zonnie – white sand, blue skies, coconuts –'

'I don't like coconut.'

'Don't be silly – everyone likes coconut.'

'Well, *I* don't.'

'OK, but I bet you've never tried fresh coconut milk, straight from the shell, have you? I don't mean from one of the brown coconuts you see here in the supermarket – I mean from a fresh green coconut that's just fallen from the tree.'

'No, and I don't suppose you have, either.'

'True, but I've heard it's the greatest tasting drink in the universe, and –'

'OK, son,' said Hal Hunt, 'I think that's enough about coconuts.' His voice then softened as he turned to Amazon. 'Your father, Roger, and I had our differences, but he's my brother, and I love him. I'm going to find him and your mother, and bring them back to you. But while I'm doing it there are some incredibly endangered animals that need you.'

That was the clincher, for Amazon. Even before she had become a Tracker she had loved animals obsessively.

'What is it that we're saving this time?' she asked, and Frazer knew that she was hooked.

'Leatherback turtles. One of the rarest species of sea turtle. They just nest in a few island beaches around the Pacific. The one you're going to is one of the most important, and it just so happens that the head man there is an old friend of mine and your father's, although I haven't heard from him in a long, long time . . .'

For a few moments Hal Hunt's eyes became misty, as he lost himself in memories of old adventures. And then he shook his head, and was back in the present, with urgent work to be done.

'The trouble is,' he continued, 'that when the eggs hatch out, most of the babies get picked off by predators before they even reach the sea. Your job is to watch out for when they hatch, and get them down to the water. You do that and you give the species a real boost. You think you're up to it?'

Amazon chewed her lip.

Turtles.

Baby turtles.

Baby turtles that needed her help.

She nodded.

Hal Hunt smiled. It wasn't something he did a lot. 'That's great, Amazon. And you can have Bluey along to babysit – er, I mean help you out with the mission.'

Bluey was a happy-go-lucky, carrot-topped Aussie in his early twenties. He had been part of the mission to save the Amur leopards. His real name was Ross Taylor, but everyone called him Bluey. He was Frazer's best friend in TRACKS.

Bluey's presence was the icing on the cake for Frazer, and he couldn't contain himself any longer. He whooped and cheered.

'This is one trip you are never going to forget.'

Flying Again

And so it was that Frazer and Amazon, accompanied by the laid-back figure of Bluey, had found themselves on another of the seemingly endless journeys that were part and parcel of life as a member of TRACKS.

From the damp and chill of Vancouver they had flown to a sunny LA. From LA they took a seven-hour flight to Tahiti, landing at Faa'a International Airport near the capital Papeete. Amazon slept for most of the flight over the Pacific, and Tahiti was shrouded by cloud as they came in, so she and Frazer had no real sense of where they were.

'Shame about the cloud,' said Bluey ruefully, as they filed sleepily off the plane. 'We just missed the second most spectacular sight in the whole of the Pacific. Giant volcanoes, huge waterfalls . . .'

Amazon used her imagination to conjure up the volcanoes and waterfalls, painting the vivid greens and frothing white water in her mind, but she still longed for the real thing.

After two and a half hours of watching the rain thrum against the airport windows, they boarded their flight to Nuku Hiva, the biggest island in the Marquesas group. Almost all of the other passengers in the small jet were Polynesians. Dark-haired, with light brown skin, some were young and attractive, others older and very much larger.

'Being super-sized is a mark of success in this culture,' Bluey whispered to Amazon, who was staring at a man so fat he flowed like lava over two seats. 'The King of Tonga – another island to the west of here – used to be the world's heaviest monarch – he weighed two hundred kilograms; what's that, about six of you, Zonnie?'

Young and old, fat and thin alike, had red and white flowers in their hair, which Amazon found very charming.

The colour and variety inside the plane were not matched by anything visible through the small windows. The Pacific is the world's greatest ocean, and for much of it there is nothing to see except the sea. And so, after a spell of gazing at the limitless expanse of blue, Amazon fell asleep again.

Frazer nudged her awake as they circled above their destination. Amazon quickly checked her chin – she'd got to know Frazer quite well in the few weeks since they'd first met, but that didn't mean she wanted him to see her with sleep-drool on her face.

'You don't want to miss this,' he said, nodding

towards the window. 'Remember how Bluey said that the view you get when you come in to land in Tahiti is the second greatest in the world?'

'I think he just said the Pacific . . .'

'Don't nit-pick, Zonnie. Well, anyway, I think he meant that *this* is the greatest.'

And then, finally taking in what was below them, she let out a gasp.

'I really hate it when the best you can say is "wow",' she said. 'But, well, wow!'

It was indeed a 'wow' view. The grand images of Tahiti that her imagination had cooked up were dwarfed by the reality of the Marquesas. High, jagged peaks, like broken green teeth, reached up into the clouds; insanely steep valleys cut their way down to the shore, where huge waves crashed into the rocks.

'It's still not exactly those blue seas and palm trees and sandy beaches . . .' said Amazon.

'Nah,' agreed Frazer. 'This is more the sort of island where you'd expect to see King Kong fighting with a dinosaur or something.'

Bluey leaned over from across the aisle.

'Like pretty well all the islands of the South Pacific, the Marquesas started life as volcanoes. Some of the others, like the Hawaiian islands, are still active, but these guys are a little older – one or two million years. That's given time and wind and water the chance to carve out those peaks and valleys. Cool, huh?'

'How come you know all this stuff, Bluey?' asked Amazon. With his long red hair and easy charm, Bluey came across like a laid-back beach bum.

'I'm halfway through my PhD on the marine life of the South Pacific,' he replied, grinning. 'That's how I got this gig.'

'Our Bluey's not just a pretty face,' laughed Frazer, for which Bluey gave him a playful thump.

'Is this where the turtles are?' Amazon asked.

'No. As you observed, Zonnie, the Marquesas don't really have the sort of beaches turtles need for their nests – they bury their eggs in the sand. I'm afraid our journey's only just begun, really.'

'You're kidding? I feel like we've already travelled halfway round the world.'

'We have – or about a third of it. The last leg is shorter, but trickier. We have to get to a coral island called Uva'avu. It's in the Disappointment Islands, a few hundred miles south of the Marquesas. It's a three-day boat ride. If we find the right boat . . .'

'Am I going deaf or did you just say the Disappointment Islands?' said Frazer incredulously.

'You got it. The Îles du Désappointement, the French call them – and remember this bit of Polynesia is all technically part of France.'

'It doesn't sound like much of a holiday destination.'

'Oh, don't worry about the name. They were given that by mariners in the eighteen hundreds, because the locals back then were a little unfriendly, and there wasn't much in the way of supplies. It's all very different now . . .'

And then the aeroplane began its dramatic descent through the clouds and craggy peaks, and the Trackers were awed into silence.

The Guide

From the airport Bluey hired an open-top jeep and drove them to the sleepy island capital of Taipivai. It was the most spectacular drive of Amazon's life – and, given that she'd recently ventured into the forests of Siberia, that was actually saying something. All around her she could see the mountains climb almost vertically up until their tops were lost in the clouds. At times the clouds flowed down the thickly forested slopes to envelop the road, like silent avalanches, drenching the hair of the passengers in something that was neither mist nor rain.

'I tell you, Amazon,' said Frazer, 'I've been to some truly stunning places in my time – I've seen the Himalayas and Mount Kilimanjaro, and the Rockies, and I've dived on the Great Barrier Reef in Australia, but I've never seen anything like this.'

There was something else that struck Amazon.

'Have you noticed that there aren't any people?' she said. 'I don't mean like a desert . . . you know, one of those places where people have *never* lived. It's as if there were once people here, but they've all gone away. Kind of spooky.'

'Yeah,' Frazer nodded. 'Now that you mention it, it does seem haunted. What's the story, Bluey?'

'It's a sad one. But I'm not the guy to tell it. The weather's too crummy for hanging out by the beach, so I'll hook you up with a guide later on while I go to charter the boat to take us on to Uva'avu. He'll give you the low-down.'

So, later that morning, Bluey left them at a little French café by the waterfront, while he went to find transportation for the final leg of the journey.

He checked his watch anxiously. 'The guide'll be here in a few minutes. Sorry to leave you, but I've got to find us that boat, and I've a feeling it won't be easy.'

Amazon wasn't quite sure what yams and cassava were, but she half expected to breakfast on them (or something similarly tropical). However, the café, like much of the island, had been greatly influenced by French culture, and so they munched their way through croissants washed down with hot chocolate. As they ate, they gazed out of the window, watching the dark clouds build over the ocean, like armies preparing for battle.

And then a reflection appeared in the window, and it was so strange and so startling that for a moment Amazon thought it was something she'd imagined, or a trick of the light. But, when she and

Fraser turned round, they discovered that it was very real indeed.

He was a giant of a man, young, tall and straight, and with muscles bulging beneath his frayed and faded T-shirt. Black eyes stared out from under a heavy brow, and his face wore a look of fierce dignity and haughty pride.

But neither his features nor his physique were what marked out the man. It was that every centimetre of visible skin was covered in intricate tattoos. Patterns of giddying complexity curled over his arms, neck, face and legs. Amazon thought that they might represent flowers and plants and animals and, as she stared, the shapes seemed almost to move, to writhe and swirl as if they were alive.

'I am Matahi,' said the man, in a voice as deep and resonant as the ocean.

'Oh, hi,' said Frazer, his voice sounding even lighter and merrier than usual in contrast to the Polynesian's dark rumble. 'You must be the guide that Bluey talked about.'

Matahi said nothing, but his head made a small movement, which seemed to indicate that yes, this was so.

'Follow,' Matahi commanded, and turned to walk out of the café.

Amazon and Frazer looked at each other.

'Are we sure this is a good idea . . .?' Amazon whispered.

'Er, yeah, I guess so. Why, don't you?'

'Oh, I don't know. It's just, well, he's a bit weird . . .'

'You mean the tattoos? That's the custom here. Lots of the people have them – you must have noticed.'

It was true – many of the native Marquesans had tattoos on their arms and faces.

'But not like him . . . And it's not just the tattoos, it's . . . well, our guide's not exactly the *cheeriest* person I've ever met.'

Frazer was about to answer, but he became aware that the tall Polynesian had returned.

'Can you ride horse?' he said.

'Yes,' Amazon replied, suddenly very interested. 'Why . . .?'

'I have,' said Matahi, and pointed outside, 'horses best for this island. Roads are not good. Petrol is much money. Come.'

And suddenly Amazon's qualms and concerns were completely forgotten. Matahi led them to a paddock just outside the town, where three scruffy horses flicked their tails at flies and munched on wet grass.

But Frazer and Amazon didn't care if the horses were scruffy. They both loved riding, although Frazer was by far the more experienced of the two. In fact, they had first truly bonded when Frazer took Amazon riding back on the Hunt farm on Long Island.

Amazon chose a grey mare and Frazer a rather

grumpy chestnut stallion, and soon they were saddled up and trotting along the dirt trails that wound up through the dense tropical forest.

5

Exploring Nuku Hiva

Once they got away from the coast, they were struck again by how the land seemed almost completely deserted. They came across many strange ruins half hidden in the trees and tangled undergrowth. There were huge stone platforms, as big as tennis courts, that Matahi said were called *rua*.

'I had no idea that there were structures like this in the South Pacific,' said Frazer. 'What were they used for?'

'Feasts. Worship. Sacrifice.'

'Sacrifice?' said Amazon. 'You mean like animals . . .?'

Matahi grunted, and kicked his horse.

A little later, they passed through an area of such dense forest that they had to lead their horses. Frazer found himself at the front. He was much bothered by the tiny, almost invisible biting flies, called *no-nos* by the locals, as well as by the dangling leaves that snagged his floppy hair and the tangles of thorns that caught his clothes.

And then, suddenly, as he swatted at visible and invisible pests, he came face to face with a demon. It loomed out of the gloom like a monstrous frog, with its wide, leering mouth, and great goggling eyes, set in a fat head on top of a squat body and short, crouching legs.

Frazer let out a yelp: he just couldn't help himself. The thing – whatever it was – made him think of the imaginary monsters that used to lurk in his wardrobe or under his bed, waiting to reach out and grab him with long, bony fingers as soon as his dad had finished tucking him in and left the room.

It could have been worse – at least he hadn't screamed – but it was enough to make the horse he was leading rear and snort.

'What is it?' said Amazon, who was a few paces behind him.

As she spoke, the strong figure of Matahi surged past her, an old but still sharp machete in his hand. Then he stopped and emitted a strange, low gurgling sound. It took Amazon a moment to realize that he was laughing. She stepped forward and finally got to see what all the fuss had been about.

The monster was a statue. Ugly and somehow malevolent, but essentially harmless, unless you believed that such things had special powers.

Frazer had just about recovered his cool.

'Who's this guy?' he asked. 'Looks a bit like one of the girls in my class . . .'

'Girl . . .?' replied the Polynesian. 'No, not a girl. He is Tiki, the first man and the father of men. The great god Tāne made him from earth mixed with blood and . . . what is the word for this?' Matahi spat on the ground.

'Spit.'

'Spit. Yes, spit. Earth and blood and spit. Or so my people once believed, before the missionaries came.'

'Earth mixed with blood and spit,' Frazer repeated. 'Nice. Anyone else hungry?'

Despite the gross image conjured up by Matahi's

words, Amazon realized she was starving. They had forgotten to bring any provisions, but Matahi brought them to a grove of fruit trees, and they ate bananas and mangoes and papaya, plucked straight from the branches.

'You thirsty?' asked Matahi when they had eaten their fill of the fruit.

Amazon and Frazer nodded eagerly, and then watched in admiration as Matahi opened up two green coconuts with a few deft cuts of his machete.

'What do you think?' asked Frazer, wiping his lips. 'Beats the heck out of Coke, doesn't it?'

Amazon was too busy gulping down the delicious liquid to respond.

The meal had been pleasant enough, but their attempts to engage the guide in conversation fell flat, so they were both happy to get moving again. They rode on through the eerily silent woods, glared at by more of the Tikis and much harassed by the *no-nos*, as well as the more usual kind of mosquitoes.

After an hour, they came to a stone-lined pit dug at the foot of one of the valleys.

'What was this used for, Matahi?' asked Frazer.

'For storing.'

'Storing what? Food?'

Matahi smiled a rather grim smile.

'In a way, yes. When there was war between the valleys, captives would be kept here. Their legs and arms would be broken so they could not escape. And then they would be killed and . . .'

'Please do not say "eaten",' said Amazon, her face filled with horror.

'Eaten? Why, yes, eaten.'

'But I thought that was all just made up by the missionaries. I mean all the stuff about cannibals . . .?'

Matahi shrugged. 'There used to be a hundred thousand Marquesans on these islands. Our culture was one of the finest in the Pacific. We built great halls and palaces, the remains of which you have seen. Our navigators sailed thousands of miles to Easter Island and Hawaii and New Zealand. Also to islands further south – one of them was my home . . .'

Matahi paused for a moment, as if remembering something deeply sad. Then he continued: 'But yes, there was also warfare between us, and if a warrior was captured by his foes he knew his fate. When the Europeans came, the warfare ended. But that was because those of us who were not killed with your guns were killed by your germs. Disease took so many. A hundred thousand became two thousand.'

Suddenly Amazon understood why the valleys seemed so silent and haunted.

'Now I will show you one of our great sacred sites. I promise you will not be . . . sorry.'

6

The Falls, and a Slippery Surprise

They mounted their horses again, and rode up a valley that started out as merely spectacular and then soon went beyond that, to a place where only mute wonder could do it justice. The valley grew deeper and deeper, until Amazon and Frazer were staring up at immense emerald walls, like the buildings of some city built by an alien civilization. The broken remains of statues, houses and temples added to the strangeness, the glory and the desolation.

Soon Amazon's neck was strained by all the craning up she was doing, so she paid attention to the delights lower down. Huge ferns reached up to caress her legs; palm trees drooped to tickle her cheeks. Branches offered ripe fruit for her to pluck, and strange, gaudy flowers for her to admire. Unfamiliar birdsong filled the valley, and an occasional flash of red or deep blue showed as one of the island's parrots flickered across their path.

After an hour, they came to an open area of

tussocky grass, almost like an English flower meadow. And it was only now that they noticed the sound that had, in fact, been getting steadily louder for some time.

'Is it the ocean, Matahi?' asked Frazer, looking puzzled. 'Only I thought that we'd come in the opposite direction, and that the sea was back that way somewhere . . .'

Matahi permitted himself a slight smile, and led on, without answering. They rounded a huge buttress protruding from the cliff, and beheld beyond it a waterfall that seemed to cascade down from heaven itself – a stream of pearlescent water, glittering with countless miniature rainbows. It was not the great spreading expanse of Niagara, but a perfect white line, like a cord linking the sky and the earth. And it fell so far and so precipitously that the water vaporized to fine spray before it reached the pool at its base.

'Oh, Matahi,' sighed Amazon, 'this really is beautiful. What is it called?'

'The *palagi* – that is, foreigners – call it Vaipo Falls, but in our tongue it is *Ahuei*.'

'I've read about this,' said Frazer. 'It's one of the highest waterfalls in the world. And it's got to be the coolest. Can we swim in that pool at the base, Matahi? I mean, it's not taboo, or forbidden or anything . . .?'

Matahi looked as if such frivolous notions as

swimming in freshwater pools would never occur to him, but he nodded, nevertheless.

'It is not taboo.'

And so Frazer and Amazon in shorts and T-shirts ran and leapt from a rock into the deep, cool waters of the pool at the foot of the graceful Ahuei Falls.

And then, as if propelled by a butt-rocket, Amazon shot out again, dripping and emitting a high-pitched yelp. Frazer bobbed up in the middle of the pool.

'What is it, Zonnie? Water too cold for you?'

Amazon was indeed shaking. But not from the cold.

'B-b-b–'

'What are you talking about?'

'B-b-b-big s-s–'

'I can't hear what you're saying. Stop jabbering, girl.'

Fury cured Amazon's stammer. 'There's a giant snake in there. And I hope it blinking well eats you!'

'There aren't any giant snakes in Polynesia,' said Frazer, although he did begin to look nervously around himself as he trod water, in a way that suggested that he wasn't entirely convinced of the truth of that statement. 'In fact,' he added, growing a little more confident, 'there aren't any snakes at all in Polynesia.'

And then the water around Frazer began to bubble and seethe, almost exactly as if it were a pan coming to the boil.

And Frazer was the egg in the middle.

Frazer may not have screamed when he saw the grim idol that Matahi had called Tiki, but now he went into panic mode, yelping and splashing and generally totally losing his cool.

'Matahi, help him!' Amazon shouted, regretting her earlier statement about the pleasure she'd take if Frazer were eaten by the snakes – and it was most definitely plural, she now saw. The bubbling was caused by a mass of writhing, pale grey creatures, long and sinuous, but also thick and immensely strong.

'Boy needs no help. These are not snakes,' said Matahi. He sat on a rock and began to peel a banana.

'Not snakes . . .?'

'Eels.'

'But those things are huge . . .'

'Giant eels.'

'But . . . but . . .'

'It's OK, Zonnie,' came a voice from the pool. Frazer had managed to recover his composure. 'They seem pretty friendly. They're nibbling at my toes, but not in an eating me kind of way. More like they're playing. You should come in, it's fun.'

Amazon looked at Matahi, who was finishing his banana.

'My people used to think that the eels were good spirits. They would feed them. Some still do. It is why they are so big. And, like the boy say, they are friendly. Take this, give.'

Matahi handed Amazon a piece of fish. She paddled back into the pool, and instantly found herself surrounded by the long, sleek eels. She held the fish under the water, and immediately they swarmed round her hand. And yet there was no piranha-like feeding frenzy. They rather politely took nibbles, each waiting their turn, like well-brought-up children.

'I guess they're used to this,' said Frazer.

When it was all finished, the giant eels slithered away into the darker depths of the pool, and Amazon and Frazer swam and dived in the clear water, washing away the grime and sweat of the day.

7

Good and Bad Luck

It was late afternoon by the time they got back into the town.

Bluey was waiting for them in the hotel lobby. He ruffled Frazer's hair, and said, 'Oh, great, I see the guide found you after all – I got some message from reception saying he'd missed you in the café.'

'He sure did find us,' replied Frazer. 'Interesting guy, in a gloomy sort of a way. Did you get hold of a boat?'

Bluey's face fell.

'Struck out. It's not really the sailing season, and there aren't any crewed yachts to hire, and none of the locals are prepared to take us out all the way to Uva'avu. They seemed to be worried about the weather, but this isn't the time of year they usually get cyclones.'

'What's a cyclone?' asked Amazon.

'I can tell you that,' said Frazer. 'It's what they have instead of hurricanes in the South Pacific. A huge storm, circling round an area of low pressure. You can see them from space. They are undoubtedly the coolest big storms in the universe.'

'Not so cool if you're caught up in one, Fraze,' smiled Bluey a little ruefully. 'I've seen whole islands that have been obliterated by one of those babies. But, like I said, it's not that time of year. Maybe the locals were just trying to drive the price up, but I've got to be careful with the TRACKS credit card.'

'What can we do?' said Amazon. 'We can't go home, can we? Not after everything you said about the baby turtles?'

'I'll keep looking,' said Bluey, not sounding too optimistic.

'You need boat to go to Uva'avu?' said Matahi, emerging from the shadows.

Bluey winced. He wasn't supposed to have revealed the name of the island to anyone outside of TRACKS. He tried to cover up his mistake by acting as if it were no big deal.

'Yeah, sure. You got one?'

'I know of a boat. There is a rich man who goes to the islands, south of here, for pearls and . . . well, he goes for many reason.'

Bluey was suddenly all ears. 'Can you arrange a meeting with this guy?'

Matahi nodded in his usual grave manner.

'But the thing is . . . I . . . er . . . it's . . .'

'A secret? We Polynesians are good at secrets. I

shall say only that you need to go south, maybe to the island of Puka-Puka, which is close and from where you get smaller boat, with luck.'

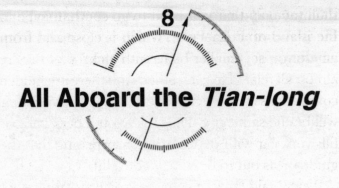

All Aboard the *Tian-long*

So it was that early the next morning the four of them took a small launch from the little harbour out to the ship, which was sitting out of sight around a headland in deeper water.

Amazon and Frazer weren't exactly delighted to find out that the grim Polynesian was going to be joining them, but Bluey said that it was his price for fixing up the deal.

'Apparently he's originally from one of the islands in that chain, and he wants to get back there.'

Amazon looked puzzled.

'But don't you think it's a bit of a coincidence? I mean the whole thing with him being our guide, just turning up like that . . .?'

Bluey smiled at her. 'One of the things you find out in places like this is that strange coincidences happen all the time. Remember, there're only a few thousand people in all these islands. It's not like New York or London where each person gets lost in the multitude, and nobody cares who or what you are. Here everyone knows who you are – apart from anything else, there are so few of them that they're almost all related to each other. And there are hidden connections everywhere. The guy that cuts your hair will be the same guy that serves you a beer later or fills your car with petrol. It's not surprising that the guide turns out to be in need of a lift.'

'Yeah,' said Frazer in an irritating way. 'You've got to get in the zone. You're not in England now, Zonnie.'

Amazon would normally have come back at Frazer with a sarcastic remark, or possibly a gentle punch in the guts, but she was already beginning to feel unwell. The islands of the Marquesas group have no protecting reefs or quiet lagoons, and soon the small launch was being tossed around in the heavy seas. Amazon hadn't spent much time afloat, and she was already beginning to feel the first inklings of seasickness.

If she'd known how bad it was going to get, she might well have jumped in the white-tipped waves and swum back to shore. To take her mind off the churning in her stomach she asked Bluey about the ship they were heading for.

'She's a modern schooner, a rich guy's plaything, really.'

Amazon didn't exactly know what a schooner was, although she thought it sounded rather romantic and old-fashioned. Frazer, however, yelped with excitement.

'A schooner . . .? You mean like a real sailing boat?' Frazer's father had told him all about his adventures years ago sailing through the Pacific, and he'd always yearned to do the same.

'Sure thing. Three masts, all the same height, rigged fore and aft. Only this is totally state-of-the-art. Computer-controlled sails, powerful supplementary engine in case we hit the doldrums, luxury cabins, the works.'

'And who does this wonder vessel belong to?' asked Amazon.

'I haven't met the guy yet. I just talked to the first mate. The owner's name is Leopold Chung. Like most of his crew, he's from the Chinese community in the Philippines. A millionaire, of course. It's incredibly good luck that he's going our way. He basically cruises around the Tuamotu Archipelago, which is where the Disappointment Islands are, buying up pearls from the local pearl farms. As long as we can get somewhere close to Uva'avu, we can hire a smaller boat for the last leg of the journey.'

They chugged round the headland and there before them lay the exquisite white form of the ship. Despite her nausea, Amazon sighed. There was something both graceful and predatory about the long, lean hull. Three tall masts towered up from the deck. The sails were still furled, and Amazon imagined how wonderful they must look when they were set and filled with the wind.

'She's stunning,' she said.

'Sure is a beaut,' said Bluey.

Matahi, standing at the back of the launch, made an uninterpretable grunting sound, deep in his throat. It sounded to Amazon as if it could have indicated either deep admiration or contempt.

Deckhands helped them with the difficult scramble up the side of the schooner. The captain was waiting to welcome them aboard.

'I am Captain Zhang. On behalf of the owner of this vessel, Mr Chung, I welcome you on board the *Tian-long*. It means, let me see, "sky dragon" in English.'

'Very cool name,' said Frazer.

'That's it,' snapped Amazon. 'If you say cool one more time, I'm pushing you in the ocean.'

'Don't mind her,' said Frazer. 'She's tame, really. I think it may be a bit of the old seasickness.' He mimed throwing up.

The captain smiled, and shook hands cordially with each of them. When he reached Amazon, he spoke a few words to her in his own language. Amazon looked at him in confusion.

'I'm sorry . . . is that Cantonese? I don't speak it.'

The captain bowed. 'Oh, I apologize. I saw that you were part Chinese, and I assumed . . . But, please, it is best that you go to your cabins until we are under way. There will be much commotion on deck, and we do not want you to have a . . . mishap.'

'What was all that about?' Frazer asked, as another member of the crew showed them down to their cabins. 'I mean, do you speak Chinese or not?'

Amazon tutted. 'I thought you knew everything about everything? There's no such thing as "speaking Chinese". There are lots of different dialects, and they're about as different as English and French. He was speaking Cantonese, which is the version of Chinese they speak around Hong Kong. My mother taught me Mandarin, which is sort of the official language, I guess.'

They each had a small, but rather elegant, cabin, lined with beautiful dark wood.

'They must have put the best part of a rainforest into this thing,' said Frazer.

'The mate told me it's all sustainably produced,' said Bluey. 'Apparently Mr Chung is big on conservation. We might even be able to get a donation out of him for TRACKS . . .'

And then they sensed a tremor run through the *Tian-long*.

'Feels to me like we're under way,' said Bluey, and the three-day voyage to the Disappointment Isles began.

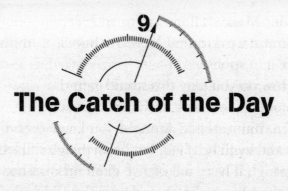

9

The Catch of the Day

And so it was that Amazon Hunt came to believe that she was dying.

'I'm not moving,' she groaned. 'Not ever again.'

It was the following day. Amazon had missed the evening meal, although the mysterious Leopold Chung was also absent. Nor had she made it for breakfast. Or lunch.

'You're getting up, and that's it,' said Frazer. 'I've got the perfect cure for seasickness.'

'If it's something I'm supposed to eat or drink, forget it. I can't even keep my own spit down. My mouth tastes like I slept with your socks in it.'

'Nice! No eating or drinking involved, I promise. It's something my dad taught me. And he said *your* dad invented it.'

Amazon's curiosity was piqued.

'OK, what is it?'

'Fish baseball.'

'Fish baseball . . .? Are you making this up?'

39

'Me? Make stuff up?' grinned Frazer.

Amazon permitted herself a small, thin-lipped smile in response.

'How do you play this stupid game?'

'Come up on deck and I'll show you.'

Ten minutes later, Amazon, her face washed, her hair and teeth brushed, but her stomach still feeling as though it were full of live giant eels, pushed her way through the hatch and up on to the deck. The sky was a thousand shades of grey, and the sea was dark and troubled, but at least it wasn't raining.

There were half a dozen members of the *Tianlong*'s crew on deck. Some were involved in unfathomable nautical activities involving ropes and pulleys; others sat or stood smoking cigarettes. None of them looked particularly friendly; but nor did they glower quite so fiercely as Matahi, who was also on deck. He was sitting with his back to the middle of the three masts, carving away at what looked to Amazon like the giant tooth of a sperm whale, which appeared to be his only possession, apart from his clothes. He did not even look up as they came on deck.

Amazon gulped and staggered, and had to hold on to the same mast to support her wobbly sea legs. Matahi muttered and shuffled round the mast to avoid her.

'See, you're feeling better already, aren't you?' said Frazer cheerfully.

Amazon noticed he was wearing a big baseball mitt.

'You know,' she said, doing her best to keep the eels from spilling out on the deck, 'that in England we play cricket, which is like baseball except you need a brain, and anyone who used a great big glove like that to help catch the ball would be considered a sissy, and get hidden down at third man or fine leg.'

'I really didn't understand a word of that, cuz, and I assume you were doing your English sarcasm thing. But I really don't mind. You're sick and I'm the doctor. Now –'

Frazer was about to explain the rules of fish baseball, but he didn't have to. Partly because the rules of fish baseball are really very simple, and partly because he was able to give a practical demonstration, which is, of course, always the best way to learn a new game. For at that moment a flying fish fizzed through the air, right in between Frazer and Amazon. Frazer threw out his gloved hand and it smacked into the baseball mitt.

It was all so totally unexpected that Amazon cried out in delight. A couple of the crew had seen what had happened and they cheered and clapped, and shouted congratulations in Cantonese.

'How . . . what . . .?' stammered Amazon.

Frazer was almost as astonished as his cousin, and stared dumbfounded at the stunned fish, caught in the webbing of the mitt.

He had been up on deck earlier and had seen the flying fish gliding over the waves. A couple of them flew right across the deck of the *Tian-long*, and it was then that Frazer had vaguely recalled what his father had told him about the game he had played as a boy. Each of the cabins was done out in a theme and, by a brilliant stroke of luck, Frazer's was baseball – there were posters of long-dead stars, along with a bat and an old sweat-darkened mitt, its leather cracked and crumbling.

Frazer was bored half to death. Bluey was busy writing up scientific notes for his PhD thesis, and the taciturn Matahi was about as much fun as a slap in the face with a wet fish. But catching fish – literally catching them – that had to help pass the time, didn't it?

So down he had gone to fetch his cousin, even though he thought fish baseball would probably never work – he even suspected that it might all have been a joke dreamed up by his dad. But then suddenly he had seen the flash of light on the scales, and here it was in his mitt. This definitely counted as one of those little moments of perfect joy.

Together Amazon and Frazer looked at the flying fish. It was about fifteen centimetres long, and a lovely iridescence played along its shining silver scales; but the truly amazing thing about it was the enormous pectoral fins, just behind its gills. They were a pale pink colour.

'They're like a swallow's wings,' said Amazon. 'Even so, I'm amazed it can get this high – the deck must be three metres above the water . . .'

'Yeah, these guys are actually pretty good fliers. They can glide for four hundred metres or more if the wind's right. It's how they escape from predators.'

'So is something chasing them?'

'Yep, must be. They don't just fly for fun. Dolphins or tuna, maybe.'

Flying fish were interesting, but dolphins were quite another matter.

'Dolphins!' Amazon squealed. 'I've never seen a dolphin. Where are they? I want to see them now!'

Suddenly she didn't feel at all seasick. Frazer's idea was working better than even he had hoped.

'Sure. I must have seen a hundred while you've been rotting in bed.'

'WHY DIDN'T YOU TELL ME!' yelled Amazon.

She ran to the side of the boat and leaned out, straining to catch a glimpse of the dolphins.

'Wait, put this on,' said Frazer, trailing after her with a life jacket. 'If Bluey comes up and sees I've let you flit about the place without a life vest on, he'll tell my dad and then I'll be grounded for *literally the rest of my life*. And unless you plan on eating him we should throw this little one back in the drink, as well.'

Amazon tutted at having to wear the jacket, but saw the sense in it: the ship carved its way gracefully through the waves, but this wasn't some huge liner or ferry that chugged along on straight lines: it rose and fell and swooped and swayed like a living thing. She was wrestling with the life jacket when another fish zipped across the deck. It was out of reach, but Amazon yelped again with excitement.

'OK, my turn with the mitt!' she said and forced Frazer to hand it over.

Several of the crew had gathered round to watch. Only the aloof Polynesian took no notice. He sat and carved his whale tooth as if he were alone in the world, or blind to it.

Two more flying fish sailed over the deck, but both were way out of reach. Amazon's efforts were greeted with more good-humoured cheering from the crew.

'This is impossible,' said Amazon, laughing.

'Well, I did it,' Frazer replied smugly.

'That was just a fluke. It flew right into your glove. In fact, it wouldn't surprise me if you'd bribed it.'

And then one of the flying fish thwacked into the back of Amazon's head with the force of a heavy punch. She staggered forward and hit the low rail round the edge of the ship. She almost fell, then half recovered her balance, her arms windmilling, but then the ship, caught by the biggest wave yet, rolled sharply.

Had she not been stunned by the fish, Amazon would probably have kept her footing, but as it was, it was the turn of the thirteen-year-old English girl to fly. And, as she fell, she screamed. She wasn't screaming merely because she was falling overboard from a sailing ship in the middle of the world's biggest and most dangerous ocean. And it wasn't even the fact that her life jacket, still unfastened, had fallen off uselessly behind her.

No: she was screaming because as she plunged downwards she caught a sudden, nightmarish vision of what it was that was hunting the flying fish.

Not dolphins.

Not tuna.

Not even sharks, although they would have been frightening enough.

This was something infinitely stranger and more nightmarish than any mere fish. These creatures were about the same size as Amazon, and coloured a vivid red. Their long, tubular bodies were flanked with undulating wings that propelled the beasts through the water at startling speed. Towards the end of each tube, two huge eyes goggled, restlessly scouring the water for prey. And ahead of the body stretched a ring of tentacles, armed with teeth that were curved like the talons of an eagle.

Amazon could see them surging under the water, like smart torpedoes, each rush sending another little group of the flying fish soaring into the air.

It would all have been fascinating were it not for the awkward fact that she was about to plunge in beside them.

As she fell, she was also vaguely aware of a flurry

of motion behind her on the boat. Frazer, she thought, making a desperate and futile lunge for her. Or perhaps one of the crew . . .

But they were all too late, too far away. The only thing that was going to save her from drowning in the cold, grey sea was that she was first going to be torn apart by these unearthly predators.

So yes, she screamed.

And then there was a terrific jolt, just before she hit the water. The wind was knocked out of her, and a second later came the shock of the cold seawater. But she also felt something gripping her. Something hugely strong. It was two brown arms.

'Do not struggle, little sister,' came the voice of Matahi. 'You are safe.'

And all around her the sea boiled with frantic flying fish, and thrashing squid in the midst of a grim battle for survival.

10

Matahi the Hero

Back on the *Tian-long*, Frazer was still rigid with shock. It had all happened so fast. The flying fish thwacking into the back of Amazon's head . . . her staggering fall. And then, as the others were still standing like dummies watching the tragedy unfold, the Polynesian had moved with superhuman speed. He had taken three quick steps towards the toppling Amazon, stooped to grab the end of one of the ropes lying coiled on the deck and dived over the edge of the boat after the girl.

Frazer stared dumbly at the space where Amazon had stood. Then he looked at the rope. It was uncoiling at a startling rate. And he realized something else. *The rope was not attached to anything.* Matahi had hold of one end, and the rope would soon unravel and disappear with him into the depths.

Frazer now sprang into action. He dived for the rope, and caught it with just a few metres left. He yelled out for help, and the crew responded: this was a situation in which a common language wasn't necessary. Frazer had time to wrap the rope three times round his wrist and arm, and brace his feet against the side of the ship, before he felt the massive jolt as the line reached its full length. He would almost certainly have been dragged overboard with Matahi and Amazon had two stout crewmen not thrown themselves on top of him.

Frazer managed to drag himself upright. He could see the two figures – the dark-skinned Matahi and the paler Amazon – being pulled along, entwined at the end of the rope. They were encased in a white foaming wake, as the schooner still made good headway.

He also saw something that made him gasp with horror. For there, leaping fully out of the water in pursuit of a flying fish, was the vivid red body and the reaching tentacles and gnashing, parrot-like beak of . . .

'Red devils!'

This was a shoal of the much-feared *diablo rojo* – the Humboldt squid, one of the most intelligent, inquisitive and ruthless predators in the ocean. Frazer had watched a TV documentary about them, and he knew that, once they were in a feeding frenzy, they would eat anything that they could get their tentacles on – including each other. He had seen what those beaks could do to flesh – divers had taken to wearing chain mail when they were in the water with them.

His brain started to work. Standard procedure in this situation would have been to take in the sails, turn on the engine, throw it into reverse, bringing the ship to a standstill as quickly as possible.

The crew had already started to do this, frantically working at the ropes and pulleys. And he heard the engine fire up, and felt the juddering shudder, as the prop bit into the water.

But Frazer saw in an instant that this was a disaster. If the ship stopped then Matahi and Amazon would be helpless in the water, until they could send out the small launch to pick them up. And by then it might well be too late . . .

He checked that the two crewmen had a good hold of the rope, then he let go, and ran to the wheelhouse. Frazer was hoping the captain would be there, but there was only the first mate and the helmsman and a small man lurking at the back in the shadows.

'Don't stop!' he yelled. 'Whatever you do, don't stop. You must keep her moving.'

The first mate, who spoke only a little English, looked puzzled.

'But girl and man . . . in water . . .?'

'Red devils. I mean Humboldt squid. All around them,' Frazer gasped. Then he did a sort of mime, trying to get the message across. 'We need to pull them clear.'

The little man at the back of the cabin looked at

him with quizzical intelligence, and then spoke sharply. The first mate's eyes widened, and he moved the engine controller from 'reverse' to 'full ahead'. He then stuck his head out of the door and screamed at the crew to stop furling the sails.

Frazer ran back to the side of the *Tian-long*, and joined the other sailors there who were trying to pull in Amazon and Matahi. Frazer saw that he was no use – the sailors were fit and sinewy from their work at sea, and he was just getting in their way. He leaned further out, and a hand drew him back. He turned – it was the captain.

'Your friends will be OK,' he said. 'So it is best if you do not join them in the sea.'

And it looked like he was right. Amazon was now clutching Matahi's neck, which left his hands free to haul them up along the rope, as the crew were drawing them in from the other end. The thrashing shoal of squid and the flying fish were falling behind.

But then Frazer saw a small group of the red devils separate off from the main mass of squid and begin to surge towards Amazon and Matahi. They were famously inquisitive, and clearly, Frazer deduced, they were determined to check out this new and interesting potential menu item.

'*Faster!*' Frazer screamed. '*Faster!*'

'What the heck?' said a familiar voice.

It was Bluey. Frazer pointed to the drama happening at the end of the rope.

'Humboldt squid . . . out there.'

'Are you sure?' Bluey replied, looking baffled. 'They normally live closer to the coast . . . And they don't usually feed by day,' he continued, as he scanned the water.

And then he also saw a red missile launch itself over the waves.

'Jeepers, you're right!' he exclaimed, and started to tear off his clothes. It was obvious to Frazer that he was planning on jumping in.

Frazer realized that it was a futile gesture, but he also understood why Bluey wanted to make it. He and Amazon were under his protection, and Frazer reckoned that he'd probably rather be torn apart by a ravening horde of squid than have to face Hal Hunt with this kind of news.

Bluey began to scramble up on to the gunwales, but the captain barked out an order, and two crewmen bundled him back down again.

'Two we can help. Three, I think not,' said the captain. 'Now we all pull.'

And so they did. Eight of them, hauling in the rope. The captain gave commands in Cantonese to set the rhythm, and soon the rope was zipping through their hands.

Frazer checked again. Matahi was tiring, but still pulled arm over arm, complementing the efforts of the crew.

For a moment Frazer thought the squid had lost interest, but then he saw a dark shadow streak under the water towards Matahi and Amazon. The Polynesian let out a strangled cry of pain.

Again Frazer could imagine what had happened. He'd observed other species of squid, and knew all about the two lethal grabbing arms that the squid could project. They were capable of holding smaller prey and dragging it back to the mouth or, with bigger victims, of tearing off strips of flesh.

This was seriously bad news. The squid were now aware that the two objects moving through their territory were most definitely food.

'Come on, guys, pull harder,' Frazer screamed. But he regretted it as soon as he turned to look at them: Bluey and the crew members had heaved themselves to the point of exhaustion and beyond.

Now Matahi and Amazon were only ten metres away. Frazer could see the immense strain on the man. He could also see the fear on Amazon's face. But it looked like it was all going to be OK. The squid were keeping pace, but had not attempted another attack. Ten metres became five, which became two. Frazer leaned over the side of the *Tian-long*, stretching down, although he knew it was futile. Matahi and Amazon were directly below him, right by the side of the ship.

And then another of the Humboldts made a dart at Matahi. Again those lethal arms shot out, and again the Polynesian strangled a cry.

And, as Frazer watched, he saw something truly astounding. The squid began to change colour. The deep red became a pattern of mottled browns, and then a bright orange, and finally returned to red. The other squid in the shoal seemed to echo these changes, and Frazer remembered something else he had heard – although it was barely credible – that the squid would sometimes communicate with each other to coordinate attacks. Could this really be about to happen now, before his eyes?

Then, as Matahi and Amazon reached the hull of the schooner, Frazer realized something else: they could not simply drag them up the side of the ship – it would batter and smash Matahi, and surely force him to let go of the rope.

'They're here,' he yelled to those hauling on the rope behind him. 'Tie it off. And we need some way of pulling them up . . .'

Matahi now looked more dead than alive. He had two jagged cuts, one on his shoulder and another on his thigh, and he was leaking blood into the ocean. It was all he could do to cling to the rope.

And the squid shoal seemed to sense it, and swooped closer again, thrashing and churning the water.

'Climb,' Frazer heard Matahi croak. 'Up my back. Up my arms.'

And then Frazer saw his cousin pull herself up the broad brown back of the Polynesian. She managed to get her foot up on his shoulder. She looked up into Frazer's face. Hope and fear met in her eyes.

Frazer stretched down again, as she reached up. Their fingers touched, separated, touched again. Frazer felt rough hands grabbing him from behind.

'I've got you,' said Bluey. 'Pull her up. You can do it, Fraze.'

Frazer gripped and pulled, and at the same time Amazon pushed up from Matahi's shoulders, and then she was hanging in the spray, dangling from Frazer's hand. Frazer thought his arm was going to be wrenched from its socket, but he held on. And pulled again with all his strength.

For a brief moment he was reminded of how they had first met, when he had helped her climb through her dorm window back at boarding school, saving her from a nasty fall. This was rather different: there weren't many red devils in England. Back then he had saved her from a broken ankle – now it was her life that was at stake.

So he ignored the pain and heaved. More arms reached down and enveloped Amazon, and she was drawn up and laid out gently on the deck.

Bluey and Frazer went to her side. The final effort had sucked away the last of her strength. She had swallowed a lot of water, and was blue with the cold. Her eyelids fluttered, and she tried to speak.

'Take it easy, Amazon,' said Bluey, and his own bright eyes were moist with tears. 'You'll be OK.'

'We've got to get her below decks and warmed

up,' said the captain, kneeling next to them. 'Mr Chung always travels with a personal physician. She will help her.'

Two deckhands lifted up Amazon's limp body. But then she began to struggle wildly.

'Matahi,' she rasped. 'Help him.'

Bluey and Frazer looked at each other, and then dashed to the side, where the rope still hung, as taught as a bowstring.

Matahi, abandoned and forgotten by them, was trying desperately to drag himself unaided up the rope, and now only his ankles were still in the water. And, horrifically, long red tentacles clutched at him, and tried to wrench him back down. Matahi's face was alternately blank with exhaustion and contorted with pain. He was on the point of letting go, and giving himself up to the red devils and his ancient watery gods.

It was Bluey this time who leaned out over the side of the ship to reach down for the rescue. But the situation was increasingly desperate and ghoulish. The squid were writhing and coiling round Matahi's legs, which ran with blood. And more were coming. Matahi looked up at him, his once impassive features now imploring for help.

Frazer felt helpless. And then he remembered something he had seen on deck, and spun to retrieve it. It was a gaff – a long stick with a hook on the end, used to help land fish, or to pull smaller boats towards the schooner. He returned to the side of the *Tian-long* just in time to see Bluey using all his lithe strength to pull up Matahi.

Frazer leaned over the side of the ship and started to jab at the squid, aiming for their eyes, or at the cruel teeth in the middle of the web of tentacles. It was working. They peeled off, some taking long strips of Matahi's skin with them.

These were mostly smaller Humboldts – as long and thick as a strong arm – but then Frazer saw something that made him utter a cry of sheer terror. It was a monstrous squid, bigger even than Matahi. It exploded through the ship's wake and soared upwards. With uncanny clarity, Frazer saw the cruel eye and the savage mouth, and the hook-rimmed suckers on the tentacles. It appeared that it was trying to envelop Matahi's whole head.

Frazer had only a split second to act. He thrust down with the gaff, aiming right into the squid's mouth. His aim was good, but the creature's great mass and momentum drove it on, so that it rode up Matahi's body, almost like a puppy jumping up at its master. Without Frazer's thrust, it would now be chewing at Matahi's face. Instead the diamond-hard beak crunched down on the wood of the gaff.

From somewhere Frazer found the strength to pivot and heave the huge squid over the gunnels and on to the deck, where it thrashed around, desperately trying to find something or someone to grasp. At the same moment Bluey finally managed to haul Matahi up out of the water. And, at last, other crew members had come to help, and carried him to the deck.

It was then that Frazer saw the full extent of the Polynesian's injuries. His legs and torso were covered in welts and gashes, and the sinister circular cuts made by the suckers and their hooks.

'He looks like someone's been at him with a giant cheese grater,' he said.

'He needs some serious medical attention,' added Bluey, panting heavily.

The captain came back up from below deck where he'd been helping to attend to Amazon.

'Ah, yes, this is bad. The girl, she is fine. But I fear for your friend here. We will do what we can.'

And then the crew carried Matahi below deck to lie in the sickbay.

Frazer looked over at the red devil. The long gaff was still buried in its mouth. One giant eye seemed to stare at the boy, holding him in a malevolent gaze. It looked, if anything, more monstrous here on the ship, out of its element.

'We should throw him back,' he said. 'He was only following his instincts.'

'Too late,' Bluey replied. 'He's gone.'

And then Frazer saw that there was no life in the eye. He was astounded to find that what he felt was sadness.

Sickbay

Amazon was checked over and given the all-clear by the doctor – a curt and rather unfriendly Chinese woman, who did not seem to think it was part of her job description to take care of stray children.

'Take this,' the doctor had said, handing her a small bottle full of a pale yellow mixture. 'One spoon, three time a day, until all gone.'

'What is it?'

'Chinese tonic. Make blood strong. You weak.'

Amazon remembered something she had learned in Siberia, where leopards and tigers were poached so that their body parts could be used in traditional Chinese medicine.

'It's not made out of tiger bones, is it?'

'Tiger bone? Stupid girl. No. Mr Chung is great animal lover. Never hurt animal. Would not let anything like that on boat. If you don't want to take, don't take. I am not doctor of girl, but of Mr Chung.'

The doctor turned to leave, but Amazon said, 'Wait. Matahi, how is he?'

'Who? Oh, you mean island man? He not good. Bad infection from cuts. We not have right medicine.'

'But . . . but . . . he'll be OK?'

The doctor shrugged and walked out of the cabin.

Until Frazer and Bluey came and told her about it, Amazon hadn't fully realized the peril she had been in from the squid. Once Matahi had grabbed her, her sole desire was to cling to his back, and everything else in the universe shrank to insignificance.

When she heard the full account of how he had sacrificed himself for her, she insisted on getting up and going to see him.

Matahi was in bed, lying on his front. His back and legs were covered in gauze. Even though they had been recently changed, the blood was already coming through, in neat red polka dots, which soon joined to form bigger, darker pools.

She knelt down, so that her face could be next to his. His eyes were shut and his breath hardly stirred. She could feel the heat radiating from his body. He was burning with fever.

'Thank you,' she said, and kissed his cheek.

Matahi opened his eyes. It took him a moment to focus. Then he smiled weakly.

'So, little sister is not hurt. Good.'

Then he closed his eyes again, and Amazon tiptoed quietly out of the room.

A Meal to Remember

The next morning Bluey, Frazer and Amazon were on deck, making the most of a brief patch of blue in between the glowering clouds. Bluey had been talking about the Humboldt squid.

'They really are amazing creatures. They only live a couple of years and yet they can grow up to two metres. They're the world champions when it comes to turning food into muscle.'

'I'll make sure I congratulate it the next time one tries to eat me,' laughed Amazon.

And then she stopped laughing. She was looking out over the sea when she saw something floating in the relative calm.

'Is that a . . .?'

'Shark,' said Frazer. 'But it's . . .'

'Dead,' said Bluey, shaking his head sadly.

It wasn't alone. The *Tian-long* was cruising through a grizzly floating field of dead sharks. Where their long, sharp dorsal fins should be there was nothing but an ugly red gash.

'What's happened?' said Amazon. '. . . I don't understand . . .'

'Soup,' said Bluey.

'What?' Amazon and Frazer exclaimed together.

'Japanese and Korean fishing boats catch the sharks for their fins. They cut the fins off and then throw the shark back in the sea, alive usually. It takes them a while to die, but die they do. Then the fins get sent off to be made into shark's fin soup.'

'What a barbarous thing to do,' said Amazon.

'And what a waste!' added Frazer. 'All this killing just for the fins.'

Bluey was looking thoughtful.

'It also explains something that was bothering me. Like I said, the Humboldts usually live in the waters along the west coast of North and South America. They shouldn't really be this far out into the Pacific. Normally, predators – and that means sharks, basically – would keep their numbers in check. But, if you take out the apex predator, then something else is going to move on in.'

'I get it,' said Frazer. 'You kill the sharks and that leaves a niche open for the squid.'

'It's a lesson we've got to learn,' said Bluey. 'You mess with the environment, and you never know what the consequences are going to be.'

'I think I've seen enough of this,' said Amazon as another once magnificent oceanic whitetip shark bumped against the prow, floating belly up. 'Let's go check on Matahi.'

At the sickbay door, however, they were stopped by the ship's doctor.

'No see,' she commanded in her usual abrupt manner. 'Too sick.'

And so, gloomily, they went to Bluey's cabin and played a rather subdued game of bridge. Then there came a knock at the door. It was the captain.

He bowed and said in his usual polite but formal way, 'For the final evening of the voyage Mr Chung has requested that you dine in his cabin.'

'We'd be honoured,' Bluey replied.

'Better dress up nice,' Frazer said to Amazon, after the captain had bowed again and left.

'Oh yes, I'll put on my finest ball gown,' she answered.

Even at the best of times Amazon wasn't a dressing-up kind of girl, and all she had with her in the TRACKS backpack were the standard-issue expedition matching khaki trousers and shirt, so she had to do the best she could with her jeans and a clean T-shirt.

Frazer had the annoying ability to look good in whatever he was wearing: he had the capacity that comes from an easy confidence, to fit in anywhere. Bluey, as ever, looked like a beach bum. He was one of those people who, the harder they try, the scruffier they look.

The three of them were shown by one of the crew to Mr Chung's quarters. The whole of the schooner was elegantly fitted out, but Mr Chung's cabin had taken it all to the next level. Everything that wasn't polished mahogany was burnished brass or gleaming chrome. There were two rooms: a bedroom and the dining/living area, dominated by a large table. The table was beautifully set, with pure white plates and heavy silver cutlery. The ship was rolling gently, and Amazon saw that there were little ridges on the table helping to keep everything in place. If the seas grew any rougher, then things could get interesting . . .

The captain, in full dress uniform, was there, as was the doctor, wearing a pretty cocktail dress, although her face remained rather aloof.

But it wasn't the cabin or the table or the captain or the doctor that captured Amazon and Frazer's attention. It was the short, stocky man who was grinning and stepping towards them – the same unprepossessing character Frazer had seen lurking in the back of the wheelhouse. There was an irrepressible energy to the figure, as if he'd been directly wired into an electric socket. It almost made Amazon hesitate when he thrust out his hand.

'Ah, little girl all better, very good, very good,' said Chung, his voice machine-gun rapid. 'Hope doctor help. She best doctor in Pacific. I had all kinds terrible disease, such as athlete's foot, verruca, varicose vein, dandruffs, bad breath, sweaty hand, baldness, she make all better with special tonic and massage.'

Then he beamed his electric energy on Frazer.

'And this is young master Frazer Hunt, animal boy, yes?'

'Pleased to m—' began Frazer, but it was hopeless.

'Big strong boy, like father. I read all about in *National Geographic* magazine. All save nice animals from bad men — rhino, tiger, all kind of monkey and ape. And Mr Blue,' he continued without pause, 'from Australia. I good friend of your president. Also good friends with English Queen, Prime Minister, President of US of A, etcetera, etcetera, etcetera.'

Mr Chung carried on talking like this all the way through dinner. There were many courses, and although some were tasty, others rather tested the good manners of the Trackers.

Frazer's least favourite dish was the sea cucumbers, which looked exactly like the normal kind of cucumber, or rather like a rubber toy version of one — which is pretty much what they tasted of.

'It's like a haddock burped into a rubber glove,' said Frazer, making Amazon giggle.

A little later came a soup with something soft and gelatinous floating in it. Amazon looked quizzically at Frazer, who in turn looked at Bluey, who just shrugged.

'This special for you, Miss Amazon,' said Chung. 'It bird nest soup. Very nice texture, you know, feel in mouth. And help make strong, like Chung!'

Then Mr Chung rolled back the sleeves of his shirt and flexed his bicep muscles for his guests. They looked like two peas stuck to a twig.

'Bird nest . . .? You don't mean that they're actually made out of birds' nests?' Amazon enquired. She couldn't see any twigs or feathers in the soup . . .

'Ah yes, nests from cave swifts. They make out of their own spit. When they put spit on wall of cave, it go hard. Then, when you cook, it go soft again. You try!'

'But isn't it cruel to take their nests? What about the eggs, and the baby swifts?'

'Oh yes,' said Chung, 'some bad people just empty out the eggs and steal nest. But these are special. These are farmed in little bird houses in Indonesia. People take nest before eggs are laid, then daddy swift make another nest. All very happy – bird, people who sell nests, people who eat nests. So, you eat!'

The whole room focused on Amazon. She put her spoon in the bowl and moved it around, as if in a trance. She lifted the spoon up to her mouth and took a sip. Luckily, she had failed to capture a bird's nest, and all she got was a mouthful of the salty soup. But she wasn't going to let on to the audience. She chewed expansively and put on a face of radiant pleasure.

'Delicious!' she said. 'It's a little pocket of heaven in my mouth.'

Chung grunted in satisfaction, and returned to his favourite topic of conversation – himself. Not that his guests minded. The one advantage of Mr Chung's hyperactive monologue was that it meant that his guests didn't have to think of anything to say. This caused Amazon to drift off for a while. She was thinking of her parents, lost somewhere in the Canadian wilderness, when she suddenly realized that Mr Chung was addressing her. And he wasn't speaking English, or the Cantonese that he used with the crew. He was speaking in clear Mandarin.

It took Amazon a couple of seconds to translate the words – her Mandarin was a little rusty. Mr Chung had said, 'I hope you are enjoying your chicken feet.'

Amazon almost replied in the same language. Then something stopped her. She wasn't quite sure what. Perhaps it was something to do with the subtle way that Chung had changed languages. Or perhaps to do with the sudden watchfulness that she thought she detected in his glance. Either way, Amazon ignored him and continued to pick at the pickled vegetables on her plate, and Chung did not ask again.

From that point on their host rather lost interest in Amazon, and directed most of his conversation towards Bluey.

'So, Mr Blue –'

'Bluey is fine. My name isn't actually Mr –'

'OK, Mr Bluey, you want go Puka-Puka in Disappointment Isles, yes? But that not where you finish, no?'

'No,' replied Bluey, trying to appear blasé, 'we're going on to another smaller island – just a tiny coral atoll.'

'And what you do when you get there? Not holiday? Save animals, yes?'

Bluey looked a little uncomfortable.

'Well, we're not really supposed to talk about –'

'No, no, quite understand, Top secret. Special agent James Bond 007 type stuff. And how you get from Puka-Puka to this other island, eh? You swim, yes? Soon get eat by shark, ha ha.'

'I've been told we can hire a boat on Puka.'

'Oh, no no no no no. I can tell you that there are no boat sail from Puka-Puka. Only have little boat, and big seas, big wind coming. Only fine ship like *Tian-long* brave enough for this. You will be stranded on Puka-Puka like Robinson Crusoe. Hope you like eat coconut, because that all they have.'

Bluey's face fell. Amazon knew what he was thinking: this was his first mission in charge, and he'd messed it up.

'But,' continued Chung, 'maybe I help. *Tian-long* not only go to Puka-Puka, but to many of Disappointment Islands. Black pearls in many place.

Chung Industries buy them all. You tell me where you want to go, and I take, no questions asked.'

Amazon could see the dilemma playing out in Bluey's normally untroubled features. It would mean abandoning the secrecy of the mission, but it might make the difference between getting to the island on time, and missing the hatching out of the baby turtles altogether.

But Amazon didn't trust Chung. She thought there was something fake about his performance this evening, that he was merely playing the buffoon.

She tried to kick Bluey under the table to warn him to be careful, but somehow Frazer's leg got in the way, and his loud 'Ow!' emerged at the same time as Bluey's, 'Why that's a very kind offer, Mr Chung. It's Uva'avu we're trying to get to. Do you know it?'

'Ah yes, know well.' Mr Chung then addressed the captain in Cantonese. The captain stood up, bowed and left.

'Captain Zhang, he navigate us to this island. I do some business with pearl, then take you back Marquesas or Puka, whichever you like. All settled, all sorted, hip hip hurray. And now for main course.'

He clapped, and in came a steward carrying a large dish with a domed silver lid. The steward put it down on the table and took off the lid with a flourish. Inside there was a stir-fry with white pieces of meat, green peppers and black beans. It smelled delicious.

'What is it?' Amazon asked.

'Chicken?' Frazer suggested.

Mr Chung erupted into a spluttering laugh, although Amazon couldn't see what was funny.

'No, not chicken,' he said, wiping his eyes. 'It giant squid fish. Same one that you pull on deck with big stick. Joke is, you see, that he want to eat your friend, but now we eat him. Ha ha ha.'

Amazon, Frazer and Bluey were very glad when they were eventually able to escape to the quiet and safety of their cabins.

13

They Reach the Island

They finally sighted Uva'avu in the middle of the next morning. The sun still hadn't emerged, and the island was a low smudge of white and green against the various greys of sea and sky. Bluey and Frazer were on deck, facing into the wind and spray at the bow, when Amazon came to join them. Her recent dunking had successfully cured her seasickness (although Frazer still claimed it was down to the fish baseball).

'That can't really be it,' said Frazer. 'It looks like you could spit from one side of it to the other, if you had the wind behind you. And you say that people actually live there?'

'It's a little bigger than it looks, but yes, there are thirty or so people there in the village.'

'But what do they live *on*?'

'Same thing they've been living on for the past thousand years: the sea, mainly. The reef is rich with fish, and then they have all the coconuts they can eat. They also grow taro and a few other vegetables, but it's true that the land isn't very fertile – it's really just sand with some rotted-down vegetation.'

'It's nothing like the Marquesas, is it, Bluey?'

'No, but it might once have been.'

'Really? Are you kidding us?'

Frazer just couldn't see how you could get from a land of high mountainous peaks to this low mound of sand.

Bluey smiled. 'This is one of the Earth's most volcanically active areas, and pretty well all Pacific islands began as volcanoes, thrown up from the sea floor. And some of these guys are huge – measured from the bottom of the ocean, Mauna Kea in Hawaii is more than ten thousand metres tall, which makes it higher than Everest. So that's always the starting point – a volcano. Then, if the volcano's in the right sort of place, a coral reef will form round its base.

'Calcium is absorbed from the water and used to build the reef. And that draws in all the other species that either feed off the coral, or shelter there, or feed off the creatures that feed off the coral. Suddenly you've got a whole ecosystem – one of the richest on the planet and, if you ask me, the most beautiful. And, as the coral is building up under the sea, the wind and the rain get to work and grind down the volcano that started it all off.

'After a while – millions of years – the volcano looks like the Marquesas – those deep valleys and jagged peaks, carved out by the rain and the streams and rivers. And, after a few more million years, all that's left of the once-mighty mountain is a low sandy island, surrounded by a shallow lagoon. Eventually, the volcano completely disappears beneath the lagoon, and the only land that's left is built up on top of the coral. So you get a ring, like a sandy doughnut, with the lagoon on the inside. That's called an atoll.'

'And what's Uva'avu?' asked Frazer. 'Has it reached the atoll stage?'

'No, it's the classic desert island: a hump of sand with palm trees, surrounded by a lagoon full of fish, and then the reef, which is like a living wall, and then the open ocean. Luckily, there's a gap in the reef, or we wouldn't be able to get to the island at all.'

'Will a big ship like this be able to get through?' asked Frazer.

'Not a chance. Even if it could squeeze through the gap, the lagoon's way too shallow and she'd run aground. We'll have to take the launch.'

Frazer, at last, noticed that something seemed to be troubling Amazon.

'What's up, Zonnie? Don't tell me the seasickness is back. Do you want me to go fetch your bucket? Or would you rather just lean over the side and feed the fish your breakfast directly?'

Amazon ignored Frazer's teasing. 'It's Mr Chung . . .' she said uncertainly. 'Do you think he's legit?'

'Legit? Hmmm . . . well, he probably rips off the islanders when he buys up their pearls. And I never want to have to eat another meal with him, but I'm pretty sure he's harmless enough. And without him we'd never have made it here, and that would be bad news for the turtles.'

At the word 'turtles' Amazon drew a sharp breath.

'What is it, Zonnie?' said Bluey, looking at her closely.

'Oh, I don't know. I'm just not convinced that he's the idiot he pretends to be. I think he was checking me out at dinner last night to see if I could speak Mandarin.'

Bluey looked thoughtful. 'Why would he do that?'

'Oh, I dunno. But then this morning I realized that I'd left my scrunchy –'

'Your *what?*' said Frazer, who was a stranger to the things that girls do with their hair.

'The thing I use to tie my hair up. So I went back to his cabin. I knocked on the door and he just said "come in", in Cantonese – I suppose he was probably expecting someone. Anyway, I know just enough Cantonese to recognize "come in". So in I went, and Mr Chung was there with his back to me, bent over his table signing papers.

'I was pretty sure my scrunchy was going to be on the floor under the table, so I went over towards it, thinking he'd look up and I could explain why I was there. But he was so into whatever he was doing that he didn't look up – he was talking to himself in that funny way of his . . . Anyway, there were various documents strewn about, and some were facing me. I glanced at one of them, not spying or anything, just, I don't know, vaguely looking in that direction.'

'Admit it, girl, you were snooping,' laughed Frazer.

'No! Well, maybe a bit. But the thing is that I recognized one of the Chinese characters on the paper.'

'I thought that you didn't understand Cantonese?' said Frazer.

'I don't – not the spoken form. But written Cantonese is more or less exactly the same as written Mandarin. It's one of the weird things about the Chinese alphabet. Most Chinese characters don't stand for a sound, like English letters, but for the thing itself. So even if the two languages pronounce it differently, the character is the same.

'Huh?' said Frazer, pretending to be dumber than he was.

'Look, it's as if in written European languages we used a picture instead of writing a word. So an English person would say the word "dog" and a French person would say the word "*chien*", but the written form would be the same – a little picture of a dog.'

'What *are* you jabbering about, Zonnie? Was there a picture of a dog on this piece of paper? I'm sorry,

I drifted off for a moment there, you were being so boring.'

'Not a dog, no. And not quite a picture, either.'

'What was it, Amazon?' asked Bluey, suddenly rather serious.

'It was the Chinese character for sea turtle.'

14

Into the Lagoon

Frazer and Bluey both stared at her. Then Bluey shook his head.

'Nah, gotta be a coincidence. He can't know anything about this. There's no way . . . not unless either of you two has blabbed . . .?'

Amazon and Frazer both exclaimed 'No!' at the same time.

'You sure you didn't let anything slip to Matahi, did you? I mean on the day you were exploring the island?'

'Not a word, I swear,' said Frazer.

'Could you have been mistaken, Amazon? About the character for turtle?'

'Yes, I suppose . . .'

Bluey paused for a moment, weighing up his options. Finally he said, 'Well, there's not much we can do about it now. We're here and we've got a job to do. But we can keep an eye out for the mysterious Mr Chung.'

And by now they could see the island clearly through the spray and low cloud. They could also see the white line of surf, where the open ocean hit the reef a couple of hundred metres off the beach. It looked rough enough to wreck any boat that tried to get through it.

'I can't see this gap you talked about,' said Frazer.

'The entrance through the reef is on the other side of the island,' came a voice from behind them, greatly startling the three Trackers. They turned to see the captain. 'We will have to anchor here, on the leeward side, where it is more sheltered. There is a small problem with the computer program that controls the steering, and we cannot risk going any closer until it is corrected. To be driven on to the reef here would be a very great inconvenience. The launch will take you round to the other side. That is also where the village is situated. Also the pearl farm, from which Mr Chung will obtain pearls. And may I ask how your friend is today?'

Amazon and Frazer had popped into the sickbay earlier that morning to check on Matahi. He was still unwell. The fever was under control, but the abrasions on his back and legs were still seeping blood and pus. He had murmured a few words to them, before the doctor had shooed them away.

'He's not great. But I don't think he's in any real danger. And he seemed very keen to get back to the island.'

The captain nodded thoughtfully. 'For the time being it is better for him to stay on the boat.'

'Good idea,' agreed Bluey. 'I don't suppose they have much in the way of medical equipment on the island.'

Although she could see that it made sense, something about this arrangement made Amazon feel rather uneasy. Was it that it almost felt as though Matahi were a hostage?

Mr Chung himself made a brief appearance to wave them off. 'Cheery-bye,' he said, grinning and nodding. 'Don't let coconut fall on head. I come soon to island when rudder better. We take good care of your friend.'

Twenty minutes later, the three Trackers were rounding the island in the launch, piloted by one of the crew. Amazon spotted a place where there were no waves breaking, and guessed it must be the gap in the reef. Beyond it she saw the lagoon, as still and calm as a pond in an English country village. A strange sort of building – a ramshackle hut on stilts – stood right in the middle of the lagoon.

'That's for the pearl fishers,' said Bluey, seeing her puzzled expression. 'They dive from there down to the bottom of the lagoon to bring up the oysters.'

Beyond the lagoon there was a strip of white sand, and behind that a line of tall palm trees. Amazon could even see the big green coconuts, clustered at the point where the leaves met the trunk.

At one edge of the beach there was a village, made up of a dozen huts. They had roofs made of palm thatch, but had no real walls – just a stout wooden pole at each corner to hold up the roof, and wooden blinds that were all pulled up. Children were playing at the edge of the water, while adults busied themselves with canoes and nets.

Well, perhaps 'busied' is the wrong word. The scene was relaxed and easy, and nobody seemed in a rush to do anything.

15

Happy Landings

The pilot steered the little launch through the gap in the reef. Looking down now, Amazon was astonished to see how perfectly clear the water was. The rough weather had stirred up the sediment outside the reef, but in here it was like an aquarium. She saw shoals of long, arrow-like fish moving through the water like shafts of frozen sunlight. Larger big-mouthed fish lurked in the shadows. And everywhere there were clusters of oyster shells, as big as soup bowls.

And then, just a few metres from the boat, a head popped up. It belonged to a teenage boy. He carried a knife between his teeth. He looked at the boat, waved, smiled – or tried to: smiling is quite tricky when you have a knife in your mouth – then he swam up to the structure on stilts in the lagoon, climbed a ladder, dragging behind him a rope hung with huge black oysters.

By now the children on the beach had noticed

them, and began shouting and laughing. The adults dropped what they were doing and started to gather together on the lagoon fringe. Amazon saw the adults talking to some of the children, who then rushed away. They reappeared, carrying armfuls of red and white flowers, just as the boat was hitting the sand.

The village men helped pull the boat up a little way on to the beach, and then offered their hands to help them down. One grave and elderly man tried to carry Amazon, but she wouldn't have it and vaulted over the side of the boat, into ankle-deep water. As soon as they were on the beach, women hung the flower garlands round their necks.

The Trackers didn't have much in the way of equipment – just the satellite phone, and the basics for sleeping and eating – but what there was, was carried from the boat by the villagers.

The pilot of the launch waited until the gear was unloaded, and then pushed the boat back into the deeper water and started up the engine. Frazer watched as the wake churned the placid water of the lagoon.

'He didn't seem to want to hang around,' he said.

'Maybe he knows something about the locals that we don't,' Amazon replied.

'I can't imagine what,' said Frazer, looking at the crowd of polite adults and shy children.

Amazon nodded in agreement. And yet she had

noticed that there was something just a little odd about the men and women of the village. True, the children grinned and laughed, as children do, but none of the adults would meet her eye.

Bluey strode forward and called out a few words of greeting in halting Polynesian, and they each tried to shake the hands of everyone in the crowd. A few of the villagers allowed their hands to be taken, but others pulled away, or found something interesting to look at in the sea ahead or the palm trees behind.

'Friendly, aren't they?' said Frazer.

'This is weird,' said Bluey. 'These people are usually incredibly hospitable. They love getting visitors. It's a mark of honour among them.' He shrugged, as if unsure what to do next. Then he added, in a whisper, 'You should keep an eye on the gear. They don't really have much concept of private property. On some of these remote islands, the people still hold possessions in common. If your neighbour's got a net and you need it, you just take it.'

As if to confirm this, a small boy put his hand in Frazer's pack, fished out his washbag, opened it and ran away with a bright red toothbrush, laughing his little head off. Frazer yelped and set off in hot pursuit. He grabbed the rascal, and they had a good-natured tussle over the toothbrush.

At last this elicited a genuine smile from the adults of the village. Amazon had already noticed in the

Marquesas that the Polynesians were incredibly relaxed with their children, and hardly disciplined them at all. How different, she thought, from her strict and stuffy boarding school back in England.

'Let him keep it, Fraze,' said Bluey. 'He'll be your friend for life.'

'Share yours, Zonnie?' Frazer asked hopefully.

'Hey, use a twig, nature boy,' she replied, laughing.

When they spoke at all, the villagers mumbled in Polynesian or French, with only a few stray words of English. However, one teenage boy stepped forward and spoke out in clear English. Amazon recognized him as the pearl diver, still wet from the lagoon. He'd ditched the knife.

'I am Oti,' he said. 'We welcome you to Uva'avu. We do not have much, but you are free to share our homes and our food. However, if you have come here to buy pearls, we cannot help you.'

Bluey looked a little puzzled. 'Sorry, I thought you knew . . . we're from an organization called TRACKS. Our chief, Mr Hunt, sent a message to your chief, Tuvali, that we would come here to help the turtles to get from the sand to the sea. And it was also arranged that we would do what we could to help you in your lives, to conserve and enjoy the richness of the sea.'

The boy looked greatly troubled. He hesitated and then translated Bluey's speech back to the others. The Polynesians then whispered together.

'I must tell you that Tuvali is . . . is not alive any more,' replied the boy. 'He –'

But it was to be a while yet before the Trackers were to find out what had become of the old chief, Tuvali, for the boy's words were cut off by a great yell, almost a war cry, and a figure of such titanic proportions exploded among them that Amazon didn't know whether to laugh or scream.

16

Huru Huru

The man who burst in among them was in truth astounding. His hugeness was not simply a matter of his stupendous girth – barely contained by his *pareo*, the richly decorated cloth tied round his middle. He was also the tallest person Amazon had ever seen, towering above them all like a monstrous ogre. Most of the villagers had small tattoos on their hands and arms, but the newcomer was covered head to foot in the same swirls and geometric designs that adorned Matahi's body. But what had appeared fascinating and rather beautiful on Matahi was only grotesque and threatening on this man.

The more that Amazon looked at him, the less funny he seemed. What at first she took to be fat, on closer inspection looked more like muscle. The overall impression of aggressive power was completed by the extraordinary contortions the man's face was undergoing, accompanying his continuing cries and shouts.

Well, not quite completed, for there in the massive sausage-like fingers was a knobbly war club, as hooked and heavy as Satan's own hockey stick.

The villagers fell silent in front of this apparition, and then shrank back, awed and terrified by the performance. Bluey pushed the two children protectively behind him. The newcomer stooped and pushed his face right into Bluey's. Compared to him, Bluey seemed like a small child.

And now Frazer could see that the newcomer was flanked on either side by two less fearsome characters, who nevertheless looked enough like the big man for Frazer to be sure that they were brothers. One wore an idiot's grin, and the other had a face as malevolent and stony as the Tiki statue they had seen back on the Marquesas.

It was a surprise when the big man spoke. His voice was rather mellow and his English was perfect.

'Pleased to meet you. I am Chief Huru Huru, and these are my people. I hope they have not been bothering you.'

'Ah, crikey, no, not at all,' said Bluey. Amazon saw that his fists had been clenched, ready to defend himself and the youngsters. Now he relaxed them. 'They've –'

'You see they are not used to meeting strangers from off the island. It is not generally permitted for outsiders to come here, other than the pearl traders who must stay offshore. I am the father of my people and I must protect them from hmmmmm . . . *contamination* with those who do not wish them well. So, please, tell me your business.'

Bluey was about to answer, but Frazer beat him to it.

'My dad sent us here to make sure as many turtles as possible get out to the open ocean. He sent a message to the old chief, Tuvali –'

Huru Huru adopted a look of theatrical sorrow. 'Ah yes, my dear, dead uncle. Sadly, Tuvali came to an untimely and tragic demise. He was sleeping under that coconut tree, yonder –' here Huru Huru pointed with the war club – 'which really was not a wise thing to do. A coconut fell from the tree and smashed open his head like an egg. A very sad business, very sad indeed. The village was in mourning for many days. I myself wept tears sufficient to fill the lagoon, as did my brothers, Moipu and Tipua.' Huru Huru pointed with the club towards the grinning idiot and the scowler.

The boy, Oti, had been whispering to the others as the chief spoke – it looked to Amazon as though he were translating the conversation. At the part where Huru Huru spoke about the death of the old chief, there was a murmur. The giant spun round with startling speed and glowered at the crowd. They instantly fell silent.

'But,' said Bluey, 'you will keep to the agreement

that was made? I mean about the turtles. The work is very important and will help your people.'

Huru Huru's face suddenly acquired a look of great cunning.

'As I said, I am the father of my people, and they are my children. All I care about is what is to their benefit. I assume that this arrangement that was reached with my lamented uncle involved some remuneration?'

'You mean money?'

'Of course I mean money. Do you think that we are savages to trade with coconuts or shells? We need money to buy essentials – medicine, corrugated iron so that the water does not pour through our roofs, radio equipment. And cheese.'

'Cheese?' said Frazer.

'Yes, I like cheese. And it is hard to get here. I would like the kind that comes in small triangles. That is the best sort.'

Bluey looked thoughtful. 'It may be that I can get my boss to agree to a payment, to help your development. But how am I to get it to you? He's in Canada . . .'

'It is quite straightforward. I, I mean *we*, have an account in a Swiss bank. It is no greatly troubling matter to arrange a transfer of money directly. I am quite happy to accept pound Sterling, US dollars, Swiss francs or euros. On behalf of my people, of course.' Huru Huru smiled ingratiatingly.

'If we have your cooperation with our mission, then I think we can come to an arrangement,' said Bluey, looking about as happy as Amazon had when trying to swallow the bird-spit soup.

'Good, good, good,' said the chief. 'But I must request that contact between you and my people be kept to a minimum. I do not want them to be corrupted by your foreign ways. Help your turtles, then leave us to our island paradise. On these terms, you may stay.'

Huru Huru looked around at the villagers, as if checking for any sign of disagreement. All he saw were downturned eyes. Except for the little boy who had taken the toothbrush. Too young yet to know fear, he gazed back at the chief. And, as he did so, he scratched his head with the toothbrush.

'What is this?' said the chief, but did not wait for an answer. Rather he simply took a couple of thumping strides over to the boy and snatched the toothbrush away.

'This is exactly the sort of thing I am trying to guard against!' he thundered. 'Such things corrupt and weaken my people.' Without further ado, he thrust the toothbrush into the top of his *pareo*, where it disappeared into the bulging folds of his midriff, like an explorer's arm sinking into quicksand.

The little boy wept, and fled into his mother's embrace.

The chief glared at the crowd, challenging

anybody to criticize his actions. Then he spoke a few harsh words to the villagers, somehow managing to make the melodious language sound like the barking of a seal, and they melted away, looking down at the ground.

Only young Oti dared to glance back quickly. He even managed a furtive smile at Amazon.

Huru Huru turned back to the Trackers. 'You may reside in that hut over there,' he said, pointing with imperial disdain to a disused and semi-derelict hut at the opposite end of the beach to the village. 'But I must insist that there is no further fraternization with my people. I do not intend to see the incident of the dental hygiene product repeated.'

Frazer stared at the tiny bit of toothbrush protruding from the chief's skirt. He really felt like grabbing it back, but he was worried that the belly might engulf him, as it had the toothbrush, and he briefly imagined the scene as Bluey and Amazon tried to haul him out.

But, he thought, *the time will come . . .*

'If this rule is broken,' continued Huru Huru, 'then I shall have you ejected from my island forthwith and without hesitation. Now goodbye.'

The chief waddled off on his huge legs, which looked like they were formed from stacks of car tyres, leaving the Trackers to carry their equipment and supplies to the hut.

17

Settling In

'This is not good,' said Bluey, shaking his head as they walked towards the hut. 'This whole mission was based on the assumption we'd have Tuvali here to help out. And he was a good friend of both your fathers . . .'

'Oh yeah, I know,' said Frazer. 'My dad told me some great stories about the times they had together. It seemed they were always saving each other's lives, sort of taking it in turns. Kinda, "Shall I save you from the giant octopus this time, or do you want to save me?" If my dad had been here . . . well, let's just say that coconut wouldn't have landed on Tuvali's head.'

All that talk of having your life saved made Amazon think of Matahi.

'I hope he's going to be OK,' she said and they all knew just who she meant.

Bluey gave her a squeeze. 'He'll be fine. That doctor back on the ship was a little hard-nosed, but she knew her stuff.'

'Hard-nosed!' said Frazer. 'You can say that again. Her nose was made out of depleted uranium, like tank shells.'

'The point is,' Bluey continued, 'that Matahi will be OK, and we just have to get on with the mission. Saving animals can be a tough business, but now you're both trained and experienced Trackers, and we're going to pull it off.'

Amazon felt a real surge of pride at the thought that she was now a fully-fledged member of TRACKS, and it helped to quell the doubts and fears she was feeling about Mr Chung, the titanic Huru Huru and the tragically lost Tuvali. And there was also the fact that thinking about the turtles was about the only way she could stop herself from worrying about her mother and father . . .

By then they had reached the hut. It didn't look in great condition from the outside. The roof was little more than gaping holes joined together by a few tattered palm leaves.

Like the other village huts, the roof was supported by stout poles, and the actual walls were formed from flimsy blinds that could be pulled up or down. They served more the function of allowing the residents a little privacy, rather than protecting them from the weather – in fact, during a tropical storm the walls would be pulled up to allow the wind to pass through the dwelling rather than blowing it away.

However, the blinds of their hut were in a terrible

state – some half up, hanging at crazy angles; others lay broken on the floor.

'Looks like a hurricane hit this place,' said Frazer.

'You realize, don't you,' said Bluey, 'that it probably did? As I keep telling you, it's not the storm season right now, but we're right in the zone for tropical cyclones, or typhoons as they call them in this part of the world.'

The inside was even worse. The floor was dusty and dirty, and strewn with dead palm leaves and other rubbish from the village. The trash had encouraged millipedes and cockroaches and other squirming creatures, which swarmed over the floor. They looked around at the chaos, each lost in their own thoughts.

'Bit of a mess,' said Amazon, 'but we'll get it sorted in no time.'

'I've a tarp in my pack we can use to cover up one of those holes,' said Bluey. 'We can kind of camp under it. It'll be fun.'

'Unless that typhoon strikes,' said Frazer. 'Then it'll be . . . *epic*. By the way, is there anything to eat around here? I'm hungry enough to eat one of those giant millipedes.'

Bluey slapped his head. 'Mr Hunt expected that we'd be looked after by the villagers. I was counting on that, so all we have are pretty basic supplies.'

'Oh no, not the spaceman food!' groaned Frazer. 'I hate that stuff.'

Amazon looked confused. 'Spaceman . . .?'

'Yeah, you know, dried soya, tubes of yeast extract. And all the trail mix you can eat. Which is fine for a couple of days, but then you never want to see another raisin for the rest of your life.'

Amazon looked out through a gap in the wall. 'There are coconuts . . .'

'Good attitude, Zonnie,' said Bluey. 'I say we explore and see what we can find. The information I've had is that there are two beaches used by the turtles – the one we're on here, with the village at one end and us at the other. The second is just round that headland. Let's scope it out and see if we can't forage up some grub while we're at it. We can unpack properly and set up our camp in here when we're done.'

'Cool, but there's something I'm bringing with me,' said Frazer, reaching into his pack. 'Matahi gave it to me on the ship. He said it might come in useful. I guess he meant for opening coconuts.'

What Frazer finally pulled out was Matahi's old machete. It managed to look lethal even when it was still in its sheath. When he drew it out, its edge glistened like starlight. But that didn't stop Amazon from giggling.

'What are you laughing at?' said Frazer, who'd expected something a bit more reverential. 'This thing is at the absolute cutting edge of, er, cutting-edge technology.'

'It's that sound you made,' said Amazon, still spluttering.

'What sound?'

'That sort of *shwiiiiiinnng* noise that you always get on the telly when anyone draws a sword out of a scabbard.'

'I didn't make any noise!' protested Frazer. 'I just took it out . . .'

'I'm afraid you did, Fraze. She's got you this time,' laughed Bluey.

'You're trying to ruin it for me. I've always wanted my own sword. I mean machete . . .'

'It's because you think you're in a film, don't you? Like you're a cross between King Arthur and Indiana Jones.'

'Oh, get lost, Amazon.'

Bluey took the long knife from Frazer. He admired the way the old blade had been ground to an edge sharp enough to shave with. He shook his head, smiled and handed the machete back to Frazer.

'I can keep it?' said Frazer, his face full of hope.

'Just you be careful with that thing, OK? I don't want you accidentally cutting off your own leg.'

Frazer, smiling, put the machete back in its sheath – only at the last second resisting the temptation to go *shwiiiiiinnng*.

18

First Trip to Turtle Beach

They left the hut and walked barefoot along the beach, in the opposite direction to the village, with the gently lapping lagoon on one side and the graceful palm trees on the other. They rounded the headland – little more than a spur of sand with a thin line of palms – and saw before them a long stretch of perfect white sand. It really was like a vision of what an ideal desert island should be like. Apart, that is, from the weather – the sky was still grey and overcast and gloomy, and the air felt heavy and ominous.

'This beach has thousands of precious eggs, just about ready to hatch out,' said Bluey. 'This is why we're here, guys.'

The beach looked flat and peaceful to Amazon – there was no indication that a miracle was about to take place underground.

'I thought we'd be able to see where they'd dug their nests,' said Frazer. 'I mean I thought there'd be a bump or something, to show where they'd laid.'

'The mother turtle doesn't do any caring once the babies are hatched out,' explained Bluey, 'but she puts a lot of effort into making sure that no predators can tell where the egg chamber is. She levels the ground off with the underside of her shell, and even flicks dry sand back over the top to camouflage it. You don't get to survive for millions of years without having a trick or two up your sleeve.'

'And I don't suppose it's plain sailing even when they hatch out,' said Amazon.

'That's right, Zonnie. Frigate birds and crabs on the beach snaffle plenty of them. That's the most dangerous part of the whole process. But even when they reach the water there are plenty of things that would gladly snack on them. Reef sharks gobble them up like popcorn. Conger eels, barracuda . . . tough-going for the little guys. But, like I said, it's getting over the beach that's the real challenge.'

'And that's why we're here,' said Frazer, swinging his machete around like a pirate cutlass for no good reason, 'to give them a fighting chance.'

Once they'd checked out the beach, they began to walk back towards their hut, this time going through the trees.

'What other sorts of creatures live on these islands?' asked Amazon, staring into the dense green of the palm forest.

'Birds mainly,' replied Bluey. 'Polynesian rats. Coconut crabs. Bugs. Not a lot else.'

Amazon was surprised. It seemed so remote and unspoiled here that she'd assumed there must be lots of wildlife.

'How come? It seems like . . . paradise.'

'You have to remember that these islands are among the most remote in the world. Unless you can fly, it's just really, really hard to reach here. Land animals have to be brought by people – which is how the rats and pigs arrived – or they have to drift here on mats of vegetation, which doesn't happen very often. And then, of course, one animal reached here and wiped out a lot of the others.'

'Let me guess,' said Amazon. 'Humans.'

'You got it. As soon as people came along, there was a mass extinction right across Polynesia. Just about everything that couldn't run or fly or swim away got eaten up, pretty quickly. Almost every island had unique species of parrot and pigeons, but most of them were hunted into oblivion.'

'So sad,' said Amazon, thinking of the bright colours and strident calls that no one would ever see or hear again.

'And it's us who have to nurture what remains. That's why we're Trackers, and that's why we're here.'

While Amazon and Bluey had been talking, Frazer had been using his machete to cut a path through the woods, even though it wasn't strictly necessary, as there was plenty of room beneath the trees. But it made Frazer happy to swipe away at the thin air and occasionally cut a twig in half. Now he announced that they'd made it through.

'Home ahead!' he cried and they all came out of the trees very close to their hut.

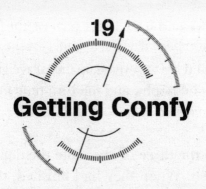

19

Getting Comfy

They saw that things had changed before they even entered. The blinds had all been fixed, and there were fresh palm leaves covering up the holes in the roof. Inside there was an even greater surprise. The floor had been swept clean, and rush mats were laid out for them. And there, in the middle of the floor, were two wooden bowls, one laden with fruit and the other with cooked fish, wrapped in banana leaves.

'Look at that!' exclaimed Frazer, his eyes as wide as the fruit bowl. 'And I thought it was going to be trail mix till we all turned into giant rabbits.'

'The villagers must have done this,' said Amazon. 'That's incredibly kind. We have to thank them . . .'

'I'm not sure we can,' said Bluey. 'Remember what the chief said about us not having any contact? They must have done all this behind his back.'

'Or under his belly . . .'

'Careful, guys, we've got to respect the culture

wherever we end up – that's part of the TRACKS philosophy.'

'Bluey,' said Frazer, eyeing up the village gifts, 'there's a time for philosophy, and there's a time for food.'

'For once,' said Amazon, 'I do believe my cousin is right.'

And so the three of them ate the delicious fruit and the fish. When they had finished, they got to work laying out their sleeping bags on the mats, hanging mosquito nets from the rafters and setting up their battery-powered lamps.

'Looks pretty good,' said Bluey, surveying their labours. 'I reckon we can be comfortable here. Maybe it'll be that holiday we promised you after all.'

'Can I call Uncle Hal on the sat phone, Bluey?' asked Amazon. Cute though the hut now looked, her mind was still on her parents in Canada. She longed to hear the news that they had turned up, unharmed.

'Sure,' said Bluey. 'I should have thought of it earlier. And you can update Mr Hunt on how we're getting on.'

'I'll get you through,' said Frazer, taking the handset out of Bluey's bag. 'These things can be a bit temperamental.'

He extended the aerial and hit some numbers.

All he got was a wall of static.

'Of course, I forgot,' he said. 'It needs a clear view of the sky to work.'

He led the way outside, and they found that the short and dramatic tropical dusk was beginning; it brought something truly incredible. The sun, which had spent all day forlornly trying to break through the clouds, now finally dipped below them. As if determined to make up for a wasted day, it spilled red fire on both the underside of the clouds and on the still water of the lagoon.

'OK,' said Amazon, 'now that's what I call a sunset. It's like looking at the world through a ruby.'

Frazer was more concerned with the sat phone. It still crackled like burning twigs.

'I guess it's this lousy weather,' he said, looking rather puzzled. 'That or the chief is so big he's blocking the signal.'

'Is it the battery?' asked Bluey.

'Nope, battery's good. I charged it up on the boat.'

Bluey saw the sadness in Amazon's face. 'Sorry, Zonnie. We'll try it again in the morning. But right now I'm pretty pooped. We've got a big day tomorrow, starting at dawn, so I suggest we all get some shut-eye.'

Frazer had also seen how upset Amazon was, but he really didn't know what to say to make her feel better. The truth was that, until her parents were found, the best they could hope for was to fill her mind with distractions.

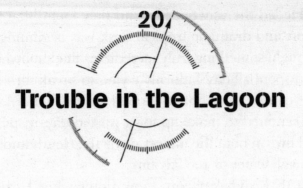

20

Trouble in the Lagoon

The next morning Amazon stepped out of the hut and into a vision of intense, almost dreamlike beauty. The dark clouds and squally rain of the day before had fled, leaving a pure blue sky so perfect it made her eyes ache and her heart sing.

The lagoon – the circle of water separating the island from the coral reef – was like glass. It reflected back the blue and added a shimmer of green, along with some darker shades where the coral reef came close to the surface.

She had woken up in the night to hear the wind lashing the coconut palms behind the beach, but now there was only the tiniest whispering sound as the air moved lazily through the long green fronds. Further down the beach, a group of children from the village were splashing on the edge of the water, while their mothers mended the fishing nets and laughed over the latest village gossip.

Soon the white coral sand would be too hot for

bare feet, but right now it oozed deliciously between Amazon's toes.

Yes, this was exactly what Amazon had hoped life on a South Sea island would be like. And yet the very perfection of the place made her feel the pain of her parents' disappearance all the more acutely. She switched on the sat phone, but got nothing but the grating static, which almost seemed to laugh at her. It was what she expected. Bluey had already tried the thing at the crack of dawn.

She told herself that her parents had been found safe and sound, and she imagined the joy of that first conversation they would have. But, like the unexpected blue sky, it just added salt to her wound.

Frazer emerged sleepily from the hut. He saw the glint in Amazon's eye and knew what was causing it. Then he had a brainwave. Bluey had already set off to watch over the other beach, leaving the younger Trackers to keep watch on things on this side of the island. They were supposed to be alert to the first sign that the baby turtles were hatching, but . . .

'You know, Zonnie, I reckon we can watch the sand perfectly well from the water.'

Amazon caught his half-smile and returned it. She knew that this was Frazer's way of trying to cheer her up, and she liked him even more for making the effort. So she made one back.

'Race you,' she said, and sprinted away over the beach towards the glassy water of the lagoon.

'Cheat!' yelled Frazer. He was right on her tail, but Amazon's head start meant that she hit the sea a second or two before him. The beach shelved gently, and Amazon's heels kicked up the spray into his face for ten strides before the water was deep enough for her to hurl herself into a flat dive.

The lagoon retained a little of its night-time coolness, but it was still the warmest ocean Amazon had ever plunged in. She came up and Frazer hit her in the face with a great sweeping armful of water.

'And to think,' he said as she counter-attacked furiously, 'that you didn't want to come here!'

The two young people fooled around for ten minutes, gradually working their way out into the middle of the lagoon, with the water now lapping round their waists. Amazon could see dozens of tiny fish, as slender as her fingers, darting under the water, but she knew that the real show was happening out on the reef itself, where the coral provided cover.

'OK,' she said, 'I admit it, this isn't so bad.'

And then things got even more exciting.

'Look!' yelled Frazer, pointing across the lagoon. 'It's a –'

'Dolphin!'

A sleek, grey-green shape rose once, twice and then disappeared again.

Amazon had been obsessed with dolphins for as long as she could remember. In her dreams sometimes she would become a dolphin, carving her way through the sea, leaping into the air, effortlessly free and happy.

'But what's it doing here?' she asked. 'I thought the lagoon was too shallow at low tide for anything that large?'

'It must have become trapped. It should be OK until the tide rises again, and it can get out over the reef, or through the gap we came through last night. In fact, I don't understand why it hasn't already found the gap. Perhaps it's fishing.'

Then the dolphin breached again, this time leaping clear of the water. And now Amazon could see that it was not alone. A miniature copy followed its every move, like a shadow on the sunlit water.

'It's a baby!' she sighed. 'And it looks like a few more dolphins are in the lagoon as well,' she said, spying some more dark shapes just below the water, and the odd fin breaking the surface. 'Do you know what kind they are?'

'Hmmm . . .' said Frazer, squinting in the sunlight. 'Well, there are several different species that live in this part of the Pacific. There are spinners and spotted and brown dolphins, and it can be hard to tell one from the other in the water. But she looks like a bottlenose – they're bigger than the others, and they're the most intelligent creatures in the sea.'

Then they were distracted by the sound of voices calling from the shore.

'We should ignore them,' said Frazer. 'I don't want

to give that Huru guy an excuse to throw us off the island. Especially not now the weather has changed . . .'

'What are they saying?' asked Amazon.

'I have no idea,' replied Frazer. 'My Polynesian is a little rusty. But it looks like we'll be finding out soon.' Two of the older children were pushing a small canoe over the sand. One, they saw, was Oti.

'I hope they're not going to try to catch the dolphins. They don't eat dolphin, do they . . .?' Amazon said, a little fearfully.

'No! Some of the people in these islands believe that the spirits of the dead become dolphins. Perhaps they think we're bothering them . . .'

A loud yackety, clicking noise drew them back to the dolphins. Up until now Amazon had thought that the mother and baby dolphin had been simply playing in the lagoon, but now she noticed that there was something strange in their behaviour. They were darting back and forth in an agitated manner, as if they were frightened.

'I think they're getting a bit panicked by all this action,' she said. 'Maybe we should head back to the beach and check out the turtle eggs.'

Before Frazer had the chance to answer, they heard excited shouting. It was the children in the canoe. As well as Oti, there was a younger girl. They were pushing the canoe along, using stout bamboo poles.

'You! Get out of the water! Climb on the boat!' said Oti.

'What? Why?' said Frazer. 'We mean the dolphins no harm.'

'There are not only dolphins in the sea. Sharks! Many of them.'

Amazon felt a cold jab of fear surge through her spine.

'Where?'

'They chase the dolphins, see.'

And Amazon realized that she'd been wrong about the dark shapes under the water. Now she could see that they moved in a completely different way to the dolphins – a sinuous, snake-like back and forth motion, rather than the undulating up and down of the sea mammals. And the tips of their vertical tails cut the surface of the lagoon, in a way that the horizontal tails of the dolphins never did.

Amazon didn't need another invitation, and in a few seconds she and Frazer were balancing in the narrow canoe. There was hardly enough room for the four of them: this wasn't one of the big, ocean-going canoes the men of the village used for fishing expeditions out beyond the reef, but a frail and fragile craft designed to be used in the shelter of the lagoon. It had a small sail made from woven palm fronds on a bamboo frame, but it was useless without the wind, and was lying flat in the bottom of the vessel, which is why the two village children had used the bamboo poles.

Amazon found that she was trembling. She was a gutsy kid, but sharks were sharks. Not as creepy, perhaps, as the ravenous Humboldt squid, but when it came to killing there was nothing more efficient in the ocean.

'Are we safe here?' she asked, holding on to Frazer for support.

'I guess so. The sharks don't seem very interested in us – they just want that calf.' Then Frazer turned to their rescuers. 'Thanks, you guys. We didn't properly introduce ourselves yesterday. I'm Frazer Hunt and this is my cousin, Amazon.'

'And I remember that you're called Oti,' said Amazon.

Oti bowed – Amazon thought he looked rather flattered that she'd remembered his name. 'This is my sister. She's called Mahina. You are pretty stupid to swim with sharks.'

'If we'd known there were sharks . . .' began Amazon, but then she remembered the dolphins. 'There must be something we could do to help them?'

Save the Dolphins

Frazer thought for a moment. 'I wonder what's stopping them from going back out through the gap in the reef . . .'

'The sharks don't allow it,' said Oti. 'See, more of them are swimming in front of it.'

What had been a confused picture was becoming clearer to Amazon. The mother and baby would make sudden darting runs towards the gap, but the sharks would not let them pass. They seemed wary of the mother, and made their lunging attacks at the little one. The mother would butt at any that came too close, but she could not force a way through to the open ocean and safety.

'Can you get the canoe over there, Oti? Maybe the sharks will clear off if we sit over the gap.'

The Polynesian boy looked doubtful. 'This is not wise. There is some danger.'

'Oh, please,' Amazon implored. 'I can't bear it if that little dolphin . . .'

Oti shrugged. 'OK. We can try.'

There was still no wind for the canoe's small sail, so Oti and Mahina used the bamboo poles to punt the canoe along.

When they reached the gap, the sharks, far from being scared off, seemed to become more excited, and gathered round this new intruder, giving Amazon her first good look at them. Some were just a little longer than her outstretched arms; others were a couple of metres from tail to nose.

Amazon shuddered. She knew that it was silly to regard any animal as evil: she understood perfectly well that all creatures were engaged in the same struggle to survive, to get enough to eat and to reproduce. But there was just something unfathomably wicked about the sharp, pointed noses, the staring eyes with their black, slit-like pupils, the mouth, half hidden, but full of pitiless teeth.

'We're lucky,' said Frazer. 'These are just reef sharks, by the look of them.'

'So they don't eat people, then?'

'Nah. They might bite your foot off if you dangled it in front of them, but that's about it.'

'I'd quite like to keep my feet, actually,' said Amazon, pulling her toes in from the edge of the canoe.

'If there was a tiger shark here,' Frazer continued, 'things would be a lot less pleasant. Hey, I've had an idea. Maybe we can use the poles to drive them away from the gap, so the dolphins can escape. What do you think, Oti?'

'We can try,' said the Polynesian boy, without much confidence. 'But we must have care. This small canoe is not good out in the big sea.'

The gap in the coral was about four metres wide. Beyond the shelter of the reef the water was choppier, and now that the canoe was in the gap it rose and fell with the waves.

Mahina gave Frazer her pole, and he and Oti jabbed them down at the sharks. It was almost impossible to hit the creatures. The sharks slipped elegantly aside from the thrusts. Oti was used to spear fishing from the canoe, and easily kept his balance, but Frazer had more trouble. Once he jabbed his pole with such force that he almost fell in among the angry sharks. He instinctively grabbed hold of Amazon, and would have dragged her into the water with him if it had not been for the quickness and agility of little Mahina, who steadied them both.

However, despite their difficulties, they had some success in at least irritating the sharks enough for them to move away.

'Come on now!' Amazon cried out to the dolphins, who had been keeping well clear of the action. 'Time to make a run for it.'

The dolphin mother seemed to be paying attention. When the last of the bigger sharks swam away, she made another of her rushes for the open sea, followed closely by the calf.

And this time it looked like they were going to make it. The sharks realized what was happening and raced back to try to catch the dolphins before they escaped, but they were too late. In a straight race, the mammals were much too quick. They were halfway through the reef opening, and Amazon had already begun to cheer.

But then something huge and ominous loomed from the seaward side of the reef. This was no foot-chewing shark. It was longer than the canoe and dwarfed the mother dolphin.

It was a tiger shark, the most feared killer in these seas. Too big to risk swimming into the lagoon at low tide, it had, with the ancient cunning of its kind, been waiting patiently outside.

And now its time had come.

It was certainly powerful enough to tackle a fully-grown bottlenose dolphin, but very few hunters will take the parent when the helpless child is up for grabs. And so the shark lunged with deadly intent towards the baby, its wide mouth gaping obscenely.

Superb swimmer though she was, the mother was moving too quickly to turn in time to protect her infant. Trapped between the wall of the reef and the jaws of the predator, the calf had nowhere left to swim. Or so Amazon thought, and her joyful shout turned into a cry of horror.

But all was not yet up for the infant dolphin. A couple of strong beats from its tail sent the little creature up and out of the water. The tiger shark's jaws closed on nothing but the surging wake.

Amazon and Frazer both gasped as the dolphin flew through the air, and landed with a splash on the shallow water – no deeper than the width of a hand – washing over the reef itself.

And there the calf was stuck. It flapped and flopped, but the sharp coral cut into its delicate skin, and soon it lay still.

The shark sensed that its victim was close. It tried to surge up on to the reef, showing Amazon the alternating light and dark stripes on its enormous back. But the calf was too far away, and the shark couldn't reach it. For a moment it seemed that the predator would be stranded on top of the reef as well. But the shark managed to thrash itself down from the reef, and rolled away, beating its long tail.

And now the calf was making a desperate bleating sound, calling out hopelessly to its mother. The mother dolphin circled round, and made her own clicks and clacks in response. But she could not come too close as the tiger was back on patrol.

And Amazon was sure she could see a new spitefulness in the great predator's look, as if it had been humiliated by the youngster's partial escape, and was now intent not so much on a meal as revenge.

The canoe had come to rest right up against the

reef. The dolphin calf was tantalizingly close, but out of reach. Amazon could not stand the plaintive calling of the baby. She had to do something. She knew that it was stupid, but she could not leave the little creature there to cut itself to ribbons on the reef or to boil and blister in the hot sun. But her brain was still working. She knew that if she tried to walk on the reef, her feet would be cut to shreds on the sharp coral.

'I'm saving that dolphin,' she said, and before the others could stop her, she picked up the useless sail from the bottom of the canoe and threw it on top of the reef. Then – accompanied by a cry of dismay from Frazer – she stepped from the flimsy canoe on to the sail. She felt her feet sink through the woven palm leaves and press on the coral, but the sail gave her just enough protection. In three quick steps she had reached the little calf.

It was so beautiful, so helpless. She knelt by its side and put her hand on its nose. It looked back at her and seemed calmed, as if it knew that she meant it no harm. Amazon would happily have spent an hour there, just gazing at this wondrous creature, but she knew that she had to work fast. Already the dolphin's skin was cut and torn, and she could almost feel the agony of the hot sun on its back. She worked her hands and then arms under its body, and lifted it up from the reef. It was heavier than she'd imagined, and she almost slipped and fell.

But Amazon was strong and, even more than that,

determined. Staggering under the weight, she made it to the edge of the reef. The mother came in close, followed not far behind by the tiger. It was now or never. Amazon hurled the baby into the sea, clear of the reef, hoping it would know to swim away with all its might.

But the calf was still dazed and confused, and it hesitated for a fatal few seconds. The tiger was on it again. But this time the mother was ready. She propelled herself like a torpedo at the shark, ramming it with a crunching force that propelled the giant fish sideways against the reef.

And then mother and baby were away, flying joyfully through the gentle waves, and no shark was ever going to catch them.

'Take that, you monster,' yelled Amazon, pumping her fist in the air.

It was a mistake.

The woven leaves that made up the sail were slippery, and coming apart in the thin layer of water that washed over the coral. Amazon stumbled backwards, half-righted herself and then overcompensated, and fell headlong into the sea, outside the reef.

She was only a few metres away from the tiger shark.

Only one thing saved Amazon: the shark was still stunned by the force of the blow from the dolphin. But already it was recovering its poise.

Amazon hit the surface, spluttering, and began to swim frantically back to the gap in the reef. At the same moment Frazer and Oti, seeing what had happened, pushed the canoe urgently through the gap and towards her.

Amazon felt something warm against her foot: she was bleeding, cut by the sharp coral as she fell. And it didn't take a shark expert to know what happened when you mixed together blood and water and sharks.

Panicking may not have been a good idea, but, unfortunately, panicking is one of those things you don't have much control over, and so Amazon beat at the water like a five-year-old thrown into the pool for the first time.

She tried to scream, but that just meant that she swallowed a bellyful of seawater. And somewhere close, she knew, the tiger shark was getting ready to attack. She'd read somewhere that, when a shark bites your leg off, you don't feel it as a pain, but more as a pulling sensation, and victims are sometimes astonished when they look down and see nothing there but a bleeding stump. She could almost feel the tugging now, and dreaded to look, in case . . .

'Amazon! Grab my hand!'

The canoe . . . it was here, so close. Frazer leaned out as far as he could, while Oti held his other arm.

It seemed to Amazon that she wasn't moving at all. She had no breath; her eyes were burning from the salt. But somehow the canoe and Amazon reached each other, and she clutched Frazer's hand. He hauled her up, and held her tightly as she coughed and sobbed. And when she looked down she was delighted to see two legs, completely and beautifully attached to the rest of her!

'I thought dolphins were supposed to save drowning sailors from sharks,' she gasped, and then she and Frazer laughed as the two Polynesian children looked on, mystified.

But then a bump alerted them to the fact that they were anything but safe. They were in a leaky canoe, afloat on the open sea without a sail and there was an angry tiger shark paying them very close attention.

Frazer's clear grey eyes clouded with concern. 'Now how the heck do we get out of this one?'

22

The Unlikeliest Saviour

At that moment they heard a sound that was the aural equivalent of cool water to a man dying of thirst. It was the *put-put-put* of the engine of the launch from the *Tian-long*. In it, as well as a couple of crew members, was Mr Chung, wearing an unnecessarily large captain's cap.

'Saved by the Admiral of the Chinese navy,' said Frazer, although he actually felt like cheering frantically.

The launch pulled up next to them – but well before that the noise of the engine had sent the tiger shark back into the depths to sulk.

'You need a little help, yes?' yelled Chung.

'Don't tell him about the shark,' said Amazon out of the corner of her mouth. 'I don't want him to know that he's saved our bacon.'

'Maybe you could give us a tow back into the lagoon,' replied Frazer. 'We've lost our sail . . .'

'Oh sure, no problem. I going that way to buy little

pearl or three from the chief here. He old chum of mine from days at Oxford and Cambridge University.'

'That guy is so full of it, you could spread him on the fields as fertilizer,' said Frazer under his breath. Then he smiled broadly, and said a hearty thanks. Frazer and Oti held on to the side of the launch as it motored into the lagoon, and then they went their separate ways with a wave.

And then Amazon remembered Matahi.

'How is M–' she began, but the launch left them behind, and they thought it best not to pursue the matter, in case the contact between the Trackers and Oti came to the attention of Huru Huru.

For the rest of the day Amazon and Frazer sat under a palm tree and watched the sand, alert for the slightest indication that the eggs might be hatching.

In normal circumstances it may not have been the most exciting pastime in the world, but, after the thrills of the morning, they were both very glad not to have anything more demanding to do.

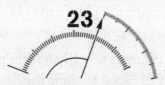

23

An Encounter with an Alien

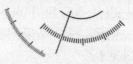

Amazon and Frazer decided against a swim the next morning, although they did see that the villagers were diving for pearls from the little platform in the lagoon.

'They're very brave,' said Amazon. 'I wouldn't go out there with a tiger shark on the prowl.'

'Indigenous people usually know the animals in their environment pretty well,' he replied. 'Their lives literally depend on it. And tiger sharks are creatures of habit. That old shark probably has habits as regular as clockwork.'

Amazon shrugged. However regular the habits of sharks, she was quite content to spend the day from dawn to dusk doing her duty watching the sand, looking out for that first flicker of flipper.

The sun shone again, although there was something, Amazon thought, strange about the quality of the air. Something heavy and unsettling, like the feeling you get when you know there's something you're supposed to do, but you can't quite remember what it is.

Again the villagers secretly left them fruit and, in the evening, Oti came to their hut.

'I have something for you,' he said to Amazon. 'It is because of the bravery you had when you helped the dolphins. I have never seen courage like this before.'

'But you don't have to –'

Then Oti thrust something into her hand, and disappeared into the darkness. When Amazon opened her hand, she found that it contained a black pearl. It was not a perfect sphere, but it was as big as a gobstopper and as heavy as mercury, and it drew in the starlight like a black hole and she put it into her pack and never told another living soul about it.

The following morning, their third on the island, dawned grey and bleak. Bluey decided that they'd swap beaches, and he walked round the headland to show Amazon and Frazer where he thought the nests were.

Amazon looked up at the brooding skies. 'OK, two days . . . is that, like, *it* for the good weather?'

'It should really be better than this,' replied Bluey. 'I don't quite get it. These are the sort of conditions you expect in typhoon season, but that should be over by now.'

'Climate change!' said Amazon and Frazer together.

'Who knows for sure?' said Bluey. 'But we're here to help the turtles, not to top up our tans.'

'That's fine talk, coming from a beach bum like you,' joshed Frazer. It got him a playful little shove from Bluey. Frazer hammed it up, staggering back into the lagoon as if he'd taken a harpoon in the chest, and finally flopping back with a splash into the water.

'I may be a beach bum,' laughed Bluey, 'but I'm still the boss of you guys, so no backchat.'

And then suddenly Bluey's face changed. He was staring at Frazer who was sitting in the warm, shallow water.

'What are you gawping at, then, Boss Bluey?' said Frazer, beginning to pick himself up.

'Don't move,' said Bluey, his whole body as tense as a leopard waiting to spring.

'Stop messing with me,' said Frazer, although there was a hint of uncertainty in his voice.

And then Amazon saw what it was that Bluey was staring at. In the water, a few metres away, there floated a strange bag with an unearthly pale purple tinge. It looked like some sort of crazy balloon, with a frill along the top.

'Is that a jellyfish?' she said.

'You'd think so, wouldn't you?' replied Bluey in an undertone. 'But it's actually a Portuguese man-of-war, which is from a completely different family. It is, however, one deeply unpleasant dude.'

'A what!' said Frazer, staring wildly around. Then he caught sight of the floating bag.

'Oh, jeepers, I hate those things. They sting like a scorpion. And it'd be just my luck to die, killed by a floating pink handbag made of jelly.'

'Just relax, Fraze – I think it's dead,' said Bluey. 'I can see it – it's drifted in between you and the beach.'

'So, if it's dead, I'm OK, yeah?'

'I wish it were that simple. The stinging cells can stay active for days. There's a kind of octopus that rips off the tentacles and uses them for self-defence.'

'How can you tell that it's dead?' said Amazon.

'You see that weird dark blue creature, on the air sac? Looks like a slug, but with those pretty feathery fingers sticking out of it?'

Then Amazon saw that what she had thought was part of the Portuguese man-of-war was, in fact, a quite separate animal, creeping slowly over the jelly-like balloon. It looked like an enamelled brooch, or a tiny bird of paradise.

'Oh yeah . . . it's actually rather beautiful.'

'It's definitely a look-don't-touch kind of animal. It's a *Glaucus* – sometimes called a sea swallow, and it's the Portuguese man-of-war's worst nightmare. It eats them, slowly. And it's also pretty unpleasant for any humans that make the mistake of picking it up – it's able to store the stinging cells from the man-of-war at the ends of those fingers, and it concentrates them, so they're even more dangerous.'

'Ah, excuse me,' said Frazer impatiently. 'I happen to be sitting in the middle of a sea full of stinging death here, while you have a nice old chat about slugs. A little help, please.'

Bluey stared into the water for a couple of seconds, and then jumped over to where Frazer crouched. He quickly pulled the machete from the scabbard on Frazer's back and with a skilful flip, he sent the gassy bag and streaming mass of tentacles sailing through the air and on to the beach.

It appeared that Bluey had accomplished this perfectly, but then one trailing tentacle, longer than the others, somehow managed to flick at him as the creature flew. Bluey gave a yelp, followed by a stream of very inventive curses. Frazer sprang up and helped him to limp out of the water.

'Oh my gosh, Bluey . . .' exclaimed Amazon when she saw the ugly red welt across Bluey's calf. It looked like he'd been flogged with a thin whip of fire. 'What can we do?'

'Feels like the little blighter stuck red-hot needles into me,' said Bluey, examining the slashing red mark on his leg. 'But I'll live. Hardly ever fatal. Best treatment is splashing it with cold saltwater . . . there we go. Not a serious stinging. I've seen guys with the red stripes all over their faces and bodies when they've got tangled up with one of these when they've been out swimming. There are actually two different species of Portuguese man-of-war. The Pacific model isn't too bad. The species that lives in the Atlantic packs a bigger punch. Let's go take a look at her.'

'Bluey,' said Frazer, a look of wonder on his face, 'you are undoubtedly one tough Aussie.'

The Portuguese man-of-war had landed in a shallow pool, formed by some dead coral. Scrunched up in the pool, it looked more than ever like an extraterrestrial. The children peered at the now half-deflated pinkish bag with its frill, almost like the wattle of flesh on a cockerel's head, at the dense area of short, intensely blue fringe 'fingers' beneath it and at the long, evil-looking tentacle, coiled like a mass of tapeworms. And the sea slug was still attached, and was still slowly munching its way across the dead Portuguese man-of-war, like a tiny, beautiful blue cow, grazing on a field.

'That is the single freakiest thing I've ever seen in my entire life,' said Amazon as she gazed at it.

'It's like some guy thunk this monster up just to give me something to have nightmares about,' said Frazer.

'You know it's not just one single animal, don't you, Fraze?' said Bluey.

'Yeah, well, I know that the sea swallow thing isn't part of it . . .'

'No, I mean the actual Portuguese man-of-war itself.'

'Not a single animal?' asked a baffled Amazon. 'Surely it must be? I mean, well, it all sticks together, and, and . . .'

'Yeah, it's pretty amazing, actually. It's halfway between a colony animal, like the little individual polyps that make coral, and something like a jellyfish, which is a true multi-celled organism. You see, the Portuguese man-of-war is really four different animals all hanging out together.' Bluey pointed with Frazer's machete. 'Here you've organism number one that makes up the gas-filled bladder. She can deflate it to sink under the water if she's attacked from above.'

'Hang on,' said Amazon, 'why does it have to be a she?'

Frazer and Bluey exchanged annoying smiles, although Bluey's transformed itself halfway through into a grimace of pain.

'If it's pretty and stings like a scorpion, it's got to be a she, right?' said Frazer. When Amazon made as if to whack him, he added, 'Kidding, kidding. But also, you know, like the way to prove that you don't pack a punch is to stop punching me.'

'OK, kids, Amazon's right. I'll stick to "it" from now on. The second type of organisms are these short, dangly guys here.' Bluey pointed to the dark blue fringe below the balloon. 'These are the digestive cells – the stomach, if you like. And this long tentacle is the killer. It's covered in stinging cells that fire a dart loaded with venom seventy per cent as potent as that of a cobra. Then they hook whatever it is they've caught – a fish, say, or an annoying kid – and draw it up until it reaches the digestive cells. All very clever. Well, except it hasn't got a brain . . .'

'Then how does it know to *do* all that?' asked Amazon, genuinely mystified.

'Each individual cell has its own job. If a fish brushes against it, the poison cell knows to fire its deadly dart, so that's what it does. When the fish is hooked, the muscle cells in the tentacle know it's time to do *their* job, which is to contract, so the fish gets pulled up to the stomach cells. When the food reaches them, they do their job, which is to get down to digesting the fish. So lots of tiny little tasks performed by cells that only have one thing to do end up with this beautiful, big, complicated organism doing beautiful, big, complicated things. OK, that's the lesson finished for today. Let's check out this turtle beach.'

But Amazon noticed how much Bluey was limping, as well as the look of pain that he was trying so hard to hide.

'I think that we should get you back to the hut for some rest,' she said.

'She's right, Bluey,' said Frazer. 'It looks to me as though that red welt is spreading.'

And so, despite his protests that he was, 'Fine, I'm fine I tell you,' Amazon and Frazer took an arm each and helped Bluey limp back to the hut.

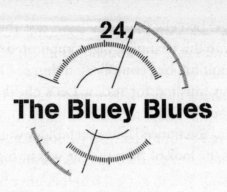

24

The Bluey Blues

It had only taken half an hour to walk round the headland to the turtle beach, but it took them the best part of an hour to drag Bluey back. By that stage his whole leg had become reddened, and even his face was flushed.

And he was becoming heavier – with each step, Amazon and Frazer had to bear more of his weight.

'This isn't . . . right,' he mumbled, as at long last they approached the hut. 'Reckon I've had an allergic reaction . . . Should take some of the antihistamine in the med kit.'

Bluey staggered over to his pack, dug out the medical kit and twisted off the top of a bottle of pills. He emptied the contents into his hand. There were just two of the small pills left.

'Should have checked this,' he said in a voice barely more than a whisper. Then he swallowed the pills and slumped down on to his mat. 'They'll kick in soon. Just need to sleep.'

'Bluey,' said Amazon, her voice full of concern, 'do you want us to get someone from the village . . .? Maybe they can help?'

Bluey shook his head. 'No, no contact. That's what the chief said. Don't want to endanger the mission. And there's nothing to worry about anyway. And just because I'm crocked doesn't mean the mission is off. I want you to get back to the other beach. I'll keep an eye on this one from here. It takes more than a slight allergic reaction to derail TRACKS. Now go!'

So, dragging their feet, and with many a backward glance, they went.

It was a horrible day, full of boredom and worry. They took it in turns to run back to check on Bluey, finding him either dozing fitfully or staring fixedly through red eyes out at the beach.

The allergy pills definitely seemed to help, but their effect gradually wore off towards the evening, and his face grew as red as his hair and sweat glistened on his forehead.

They finally came back at sunset and found him fast asleep. They tucked him up, and then Frazer went outside to try again with the sat phone.

'This is dumb, dumb, dumb,' he spat when all he got was the now familiar static. 'Either it's bust or there's someone trying to jam it. If I'd have got through, I'd definitely have asked Dad to sort out a medical evac. This has all gone too far. You said before that I like to pretend I'm in a movie . . . Well, maybe I do, but this is the wrong sort of picture. It's like a zombie apocalypse.'

'There's no point raving like a madman,' Amazon said. 'We've got to work with what we've got. I say we go and ask at the village for some more allergy pills. I know Bluey's against it, but I don't think he's thinking straight.'

Frazer nodded. 'OK, I'm sick of doing nothing but watching sand all day. And I bet big chief Huru Huru has every medication under the sun, all paid for with that Swiss bank account.'

So together they set off towards the village.

Once again a grey day had died in an unexpected blaze of glory. By now the last of the sunset had burned itself out, and the sudden deep black of the tropical night had fallen. A few hundred metres away, on the other side of the beach, the low orange light of small fires glowed through the small windows of the village huts, and even showed through the flimsy walls. It was a target to aim for.

They reached the village and found the open spaces utterly deserted. No children played outside. No neighbours chatted in front of open doors.

'Kind of spooky,' said Frazer in a hushed tone.

Amazon marched up to one neatly kept hut. She looked for something solid to knock, but nothing seemed suitable: the walls were made of matting, and the poles holding up the roof just didn't seem to be the kinds of things that you knocked on. So she cleared her throat and said, 'Excuse me, I mean, *excusez-moi*.'

She heard the sound of whispering within. But nobody came to the door. She tried another hut, with the same result.

'We need medicine for a sick man,' she said. 'Er, *nous avons besoin de médicaments*.'

Still there was nothing, and then even the light within the hut was extinguished.

'What is the meaning of this?'

The voice, deep and rumbling, made them both leap in the air. It was Huru Huru, and he looked even more terrifying than usual, with his tattoos and huge size both somehow exaggerated by the starlight.

'Hello, Mr Huru,' said Frazer once he'd overcome his surprise. 'Our friend Bluey is in a bad way. He needs some allergy pills. We were hoping that –'

'You were warned!' boomed the giant. 'No contact with my people. That was the simple request. And yet here you are.'

'But it's an emergency,' cried Amazon.

'And what, girl, would happen if you use up our meagre supplies of medicine, and then one of our village children falls ill? How do you think my people would feel about you taking the medicine from the very lips of their children? I can tell you now that I am not responsible for the actions of an angry parent . . .'

Then Amazon noticed, for the first time, that Huru Huru's war club was swinging in his mighty grip. The threat was clear, and it did not come from the frightened villagers. She suddenly knew in her soul that the chief was a very dangerous man indeed. The sort of man who would kill to get what he wanted.

'Come on,' she said to Frazer. And, when he looked like he wanted to argue the point with Huru Huru, she grabbed his sleeve and dragged him away.

Frazer knew better than to argue in front of the big chief, but, as soon as they were out of earshot, he turned to remonstrate with her.

'We need that medicine,' he said in an urgent whisper.

'And,' came a voice from close by, 'I will help you get it. But not tonight. Tomorrow.'

'Tomorrow!' gasped Frazer. 'But Bluey needs help now . . .'

'Tonight it is too dangerous. Huru Huru is prowling. It must be tomorrow.'

And then little Oti, who had followed them silently from the village, told them his plan.

25

The Hatchlings

The next day was filled with joy and unhappiness. The unhappiness came from Bluey. The children hoped he would somehow be better when he woke up in the morning, but he was worse. They wanted to stay with him, but he insisted that they fulfil their mission.

'I'll get well in the end,' he rasped, 'but the baby turtles only have one chance, and you're it.'

So once again they spent their time running between the two beaches and the hut as the day grew heavy and humid.

Amazon had just returned to the turtle beach with the report that Bluey had drifted back into sleep when she saw something rather strange happen out on the rippled dune. At first she thought it was just heat haze, or perhaps a mysterious breeze stirring up the sand. But then she saw a definite little plume of sand erupt from the surface.

'Fraze . . .' she said.

'What? I wasn't asleep, I was just resting my eyes. Who . . .? Where . . .?'

'I think it's beginning,' Amazon continued. 'Come on.'

Together they ran over to the patch of dune Amazon had witnessed stirring. They got there just in time to see the first baby turtle emerge. It was hardly bigger than the circle made by Amazon's thumb and forefinger. Amazon could not resist a squeal of pure pleasure. Suddenly all the other problems disappeared into the background, and all that existed was this patch of sand and these tiny creatures, struggling for dear life.

Amazon and Frazer looked at each other. He smiled and said, 'You do the first one, Zonnie. You've earned it, with all that puking you did on the boat.'

Without another word, Amazon picked up the little turtle. It flapped its disproportionately large flippers, almost like a baby bird stretching its wings, and Amazon nearly dropped it. But then she cupped it more securely in her hands and ran the twenty metres down to the sea. She waded out until the water lapped round her knees, and gently released the turtle. It bobbed on the surface for a few strokes and then dived down. Amazon lingered, trying to catch another glimpse, but it was gone forever into the infinite blue.

She turned back and saw that Frazer was right behind her, carrying half a dozen of the babies in the untucked front of his shirt.

'They're coming thick and fast,' he said, his face wearing a smile so wide it reached his ears.

As thirteen-year-olds go, Amazon thought that Frazer was pretty mature. But the joy of the moment had transformed him back into a carefree boy, playing on the beach.

Amazon raced past him. Three more of the babies were already trundling down the dunes. She scooped them up and raced back to the water, her bare feet hardly touching the hot sand. Frazer's smile had gone when she reached him. He pointed into the sky.

'Frigate birds,' he said. 'Sky pirates. A baby turtle's worst nightmare.'

Amazon looked up and saw four of the great black birds circling just above their heads.

Amazon had seen the frigate birds many times as they soared over the island. They were impressive and formidable birds, but she found it hard to love them. Like flying pirates, they harried the other seabirds, especially Amazon's favourites – the beautiful and graceful red-tailed tropicbirds – trying to get them to drop the fish they'd caught. With a professional naturalist's eye, she would marvel at the way the frigates could suddenly change direction and then catch the dropped fish in mid-air. But still her heart used to exult when the much smaller tropicbirds escaped.

Now she was seeing the frigates from close up as they swooped to within a metre of her. With long wings, like black scythes, great hooked beaks and vivid blood-red throat patches, they really were impressive and rather frightening.

Urgently now, Amazon and Frazer ferried the turtles. They decided that the best way was for Amazon to carry them halfway, where she handed over to Frazer, who took them down to the water. That way she was always close enough to ward off the birds. It was exhausting, but also exciting: for the first time since the mission to help the Amur leopards in Siberia, Amazon felt that she was a true Tracker, genuinely making a difference.

At the busiest moment, when the turtles were bursting through the surface almost too quickly for them to grab, Amazon looked up and saw two figures standing in the shade of the palms fringing the beach.

'Is that . . .?'

'Yep, the big guy's brothers, Moipu and Tipua.'

'Can you help us?' Amazon called out, partly because some help would come in very handy right now, but also because she wanted to include some of the islanders in their mission. But, without a word, the two men disappeared back into the dense shade.

The two Trackers looked at each other, shrugged and got on with the job. And they didn't lose a single turtle to the swooping, snapping frigates, or to the little crabs that emerged from burrows in the sand, eager for their share of the feast. They counted a hundred and fifty babies, although in the panic and rush it was hard to be accurate.

After the final turtle had been safely conveyed to the ocean, Amazon and Frazer plopped down on to the sand.

'I am totally pooped,' said Amazon.

'Me too. Er, pooped means tired in England too, yeah?'

Amazon was almost too tired to laugh.

They waited until the sun began to set, but no more nests hatched out. It was time to get back to check on Bluey.

Plus, there was a whole new adventure to be had that evening.

26

Attacked from Above

They began to walk towards the lights and then, heading for their rendezvous, drifted to the deeper cover of the treeline. Amazon was startled to see just how dark it had become in such a short time. Not long before, the sunset had set the ocean on fire, but now the world was as black as her precious pearl. There may have been stars, but the thick cloud hid them.

Once they were among the trees, the bugs started to home in on them. Amazon slapped vainly at her face.

'Here,' said Frazer. 'Jungle formula. Might help a little.'

'Thanks. For our next adventure can we go somewhere without bugs? They really bug me, bugs.'

'OK. I'll make sure Dad sends us to the South Pole.'

'That'll do. I love penguins.'

'Ouch!'

'What?'

'Tree root. It's as black as a black cat's butt in a black hole during an eclipse.'

'Have you got your torch?'

'Yep, but you know that Oti said not to use it unless there's an emergency – OW!'

'Another tree root?'

'No, stone, I think. Wait, what the heck . . . it's moving. It's ALIVE!'

Frazer now fumbled frantically for his small but powerful torch.

'OK, I say it's an emergency!' he said and shone the beam on the ground. Then he yelped, and did a high-stepping dance that Amazon would have found hysterical had she not seen what was on the floor beneath his feet: the ground was swarming with dozens of the most enormous crabs she had ever seen, scurrying away from the beam of Frazer's torch. They were the size of bowling balls, and had huge claws that looked just about able to crack open a bowling ball. In fact, that's exactly what some of them seemed to be trying to do.

'What are they carrying? Not coconuts, surely?'

'Yeah,' said Frazer, shining his torch around. 'And look, they're climbing up into the trees. Do you think maybe we're actually asleep and dreaming this?'

At that moment something thudded into the ground at Amazon's feet.

'Time to get out of here,' said Frazer. 'I've remembered what these are.'

He grabbed Amazon's hand and dragged her from under the coconut palms. It was in the nick of time. Another of the heavy coconuts landed right where she had been standing.

'That would have –'

'Killed you. Dead right. More people die from being hit on the head by falling coconuts than . . . than . . .'

'Than what?'

'I can't remember. Maybe it's being eaten by crocodiles. Or sharks. Or maybe it's being struck by lightning. Or –'

'Are you sure it's not that more people are killed by coconuts landing on their heads than any other nut? I know peanuts can be quite dangerous . . .'

'Funny,' said Frazer. 'Next time I'll leave you to get brained by the coconut. See who's laughing then.'

'So what are those things, then?' asked Amazon.

'Coconut crabs. They eat –'

'Coconuts, I get it.'

'Very interesting species, actually,' said Frazer. 'They're the only animal capable of breaking into a coconut. They climb the palm trees, snip off a coconut, let it fall and then carry it back into the jungle. Apparently they taste very nice themselves . . .'

'Lucky for them we've eaten.'

Amazon and Frazer crept along the edge of the jungle, watching out carefully for both the crabs on the ground and the coconuts in the trees. In ten minutes they reached the outskirts of the village.

'So far,' came a voice from the darkness, 'I believe you are the worst burglars I have ever seen – or heard.'

27

The House of Huru Huru

Amazon and Frazer spun round, and Frazer aimed the beam of his torch at the voice. It belonged, they were relieved to see, to Oti.

'How long have you been spying on us?' Amazon was a little annoyed about the boy's low opinion of her skills as a burglar.

'Spying? No. I have just come. But I could have heard you from across the lagoon. It is lucky that the other villagers are afraid of the dark, and dread the restless spirits of the dead that roam the jungle in the night, otherwise they would have come to see what all the commotion was about, and then our plan would have been revealed.'

'And why aren't you afraid of the dark?'

'It is for the same reason that I speak English. My parents were drowned in an accident at sea, and so my uncle arranged for me to go to school in Tonga. I was not happy, but they gave me English words, and took away my island fears.'

'Who is your uncle?'

'My uncle was Tuvali, who some called Omo.'

'The old chief? The one who died?'

Oti looked bitter and almost hissed. 'The one who was killed.'

'KILLED!' exclaimed Amazon.

'You mean murdered . . .? But that's terrible. By Huru Huru? I thought he was his nephew?'

'Pah! Huru Huru is not his nephew. That is just another of his lies. And since the death of Tuvali everyone in the village is terrified. They know that Huru Huru and his brothers will kill anyone who gets in their way – man, woman or child.'

'OK,' said Frazer. 'This is getting nastier by the minute. What shall we do?'

Amazon's face was set in a stern mask of determination. 'We've no choice – we have to go on.' She turned to Oti. 'I'm sorry for the death of your uncle. But we need that medicine, and you're our only hope of getting it . . .'

He nodded. 'Follow me.'

Oti led them behind the village, where they came to a path through the jungle.

'Huru Huru does not live with the other villagers,' explained the Polynesian boy. 'He lives in the house of the old missionary who used to live on the island. The missionary was old and used to drink much strong spirits, and so Huru Huru said to him, "We have no need of you now. We are better men than you." He sent him to live in the small hut where you are now staying, but he did not like it, and so he died.'

'There seems to be a lot of dying on your island,' said Frazer ruefully.

'There is much dying since the coming of Huru Huru.'

The path rose gently for a couple of hundred metres, and then they reached a clearing. In the middle of it there was a single-storey house, built on the European rather than Polynesian model. Amazon was amazed to see that it glowed with electric light. And then she heard the hum of a generator.

The three of them crouched in the darkness and Oti went over the plan one more time.

'I will go to the door and make an enquiry of the chief. While Huru Huru is talking to me, you must go to the back of the house and climb through the window. The woman who cleans and cooks for Huru Huru has told me that the medicine is all kept in the bathroom. You must be quick. I will talk with the chief for as long as I can, but if he catches you, it will not be pleasant.'

'Who does the chief live with?' Amazon asked.

'Nobody could live with Huru Huru. There were four wives, but they all ran away. Far away. Not even the dogs will live with him.'

'So,' said Amazon, returning to the point she wanted to make, 'if he lives alone, who is that talking?'

The other two now began to listen intently. And, yes, the sound of voices was coming from the house. One of the voices was Huru Huru's. The other was also vaguely familiar.

They exchanged glances and Frazer nodded towards an open window. 'Let's go have a closer look.'

Oti shook his head. 'It is not safe! We have a plan that we should stick to. Or else we should go away. Huru Huru is not a man to be taken lightly . . .'

But Frazer was already crawling, commando-style, towards the house. Amazon shrugged, rolled her eyes and followed him, experiencing one of those rare moments when she half wished she were back at her old school in England.

They reached the veranda. Frazer looked around. There was no sign of Oti.

'I never figured that kid to be yellow,' he whispered.

'It's different for him,' Amazon replied. 'He has to live here. We're just visitors, remember.'

Frazer shrugged. 'Guess so. Anyway, it doesn't matter now. I just want to have a look-see what's going on, then maybe we can try to sneak in without Oti's diversion.'

And then he led the way silently until they were right under the window. Now the voices were perfectly clear. They were speaking English, although one of the voices carried a strong Chinese accent. And there were sounds of eating – messy eating . . .

'And do we know when the rest of them come out?'

'It can be hard to say, exactly.'

'Exactly mean what? Can you say within a day either side?'

'Possibly.'

When the other person replied, his voice was quite different: it was clear and cold and incisive, and it sent a chill through the listeners.

'Stop playing the innocent, Huru Huru. You only remain the chief here because I tolerate it. I could wipe out you and your village with a click of my fingers.'

Amazon looked at Frazer, and an unspoken word passed between them. They both peeked up just above the window ledge. And there, before them, they saw the titanic Huru Huru spooning a thick stew into his mouth. And opposite him was Leopold Chung, looking as impish and slippery as ever.

Huru Huru paused for a moment before answering Chung. He wiped his mouth on a napkin and then said, slowly, 'Perhaps you could. Perhaps you couldn't. But even if you did then who would supply you with your pearls, and your other little pets, hmmm? You would be biting off your tongue to spite your face, as the English say. It simply would not make sense.'

Chung smiled, and when he spoke again the buffoonish Chung was back.

'When you rich as me, you don't need make sense. Money buy all sense I need. I got fifty men work for me with more sense than you got in little finger.'

'I don't doubt it.'

'I just want straight answer,' said Chung. 'The first one has gone – you said your brothers saw. That's not so bad, as long as we get rest.'

Amazon and Frazer looked at each other, and each saw reflected in the other their own shock and surprise. This, surely, could only mean one thing, and together they silently mouthed the word: 'TURTLES!'

'OK, my friend,' replied Huru Huru. 'I will give you my best guess, based on what I have observed. I think the first was a fluke. I would say it will be two days before the others emerge. I would not care to bet my life on it, but that is my best estimate.'

'Two day not so long. I wait. Now we eat more of stew. This beef?'

'Beef? How on earth could I obtain beef on an island like this? No, no, no. Guess again.'

'It lamb?'

Huru Huru shook his enormous head.

'OK, I give in. What meat?'

'Why, it is turtle, of course. In your honour, my friend. But do not worry: I permitted her to lay her eggs before I killed her. Even I would not allow the delights of eating one of the world's rarest delicacies to get in the way of making a good profit.'

Neither Amazon nor Frazer would later admit to being the one who gasped audibly. Perhaps they both made a sound that would have been inaudible alone but, magnified by a factor of two, it just popped into the range detectable by the human ear. In any case it was loud enough for the heads of Huru Huru and Leopold Chung to spin in their direction. And, as they spun, Chung, with a speed that they could not have anticipated, drew an automatic pistol from under the table.

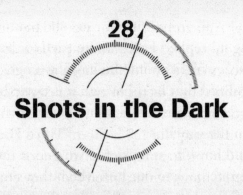
Shots in the Dark

'Run,' hissed Frazer and the two of them sped away across the clearing, keeping as low to the ground as they could. They hit the bushes a second before a loud bang came from the house. Amazon sensed the leaves above her head shudder as a bullet passed through them. She expected to feel fear, but what she actually felt was indignation. She wanted to shout out: 'How dare you fire real bullets at us! We're only kids. It's not fair!'

That she didn't was due partly to the realization that that would be insane, but more to the fact that Frazer was dragging her along behind him. Branches whipped at their faces and vines caught their legs, but still they ran blindly on.

Another shot rang out, and some guttural curse or command in Chinese followed it. Then, to Amazon's horror, she heard an answering shout coming from the trees to their right. And then, even more dismayingly, from their left.

'They're all around us, Frazer,' she panted.

'Dang it,' replied Frazer as he tried to drag some of the heavy night air into his gasping lungs. 'Should have realized that he'd have guards posted around the place. We must have struck lucky and missed them on the way in.'

'Would have been luckier if we'd seen them and simply gone back to our hut. Maybe we should just give ourselves up and explain. I mean we didn't do anything wrong. At least nothing that deserves getting shot at.'

'There's no way I'm handing myself in to those madmen. If Huru Huru would eat endangered turtles, he'd probably eat us as well. And Chung is about as stable as a one-legged man trying to pick his nose with his toe during an earthquake.'

They heard the voices getting closer, and the sounds of heavy feet crunching through the undergrowth. Amazon opened her lips to speak again. The words, however, never emerged. A hand closed over her mouth, silencing both the words and the scream that would have taken their place.

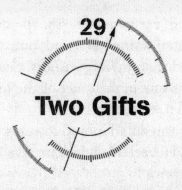

29

Two Gifts

'Do not move or make a sound,' said Oti's voice in her ear.

Amazon relaxed and the boy released her.

'Do that again and I'll, well, I don't know what I'll do. Just don't do it again. I hate being sneaked up on.'

Frazer had seen what was happening and moved close to them.

'What . . .? Where . . .?' he began, but Oti put his finger to his lips.

'Stay. I will run. I know these woods. They will not catch me. But you must be as silent as the spirits of the dead. When they follow me, you must go that way.' Oti pointed into the darkness. 'You will find the path. Go home. Oh, and take this.'

Then the young Polynesian crammed something into Amazon's hand and, without another word, ran towards the approaching voices. He made no attempt to move quietly, but crashed through the undergrowth like a startled boar.

Voices were raised again. Sharp commands in Chinese. Then someone cried out, 'STOP!' in English. And then three gunshots, deafening and somehow obscene in the quiet of the forest. Frazer saw the flash from the barrel.

Amazon gasped and moved towards the noise.

'No,' said Frazer. 'He'll be fine. We'll just get in the way. Come on.'

And then he took her free hand and led her through the dark trees, until they reached the path. Two more shots rang out before they reached it, but each one seemed, strangely, to bring them hope – it meant that the Polynesian was still running, still alive.

They would probably have walked right past the path had the clouds not picked that moment to part. There was a sliver of moon, and beyond it a shimmering ocean of stars, which provided just enough light for them to see their way. In ten minutes they reached the village. They skirted it, and then ran along the edge of the beach until they found their hut. They got there just as the clouds closed again, turning out the faint light of the moon and stars. Bluey was still snoring gently, under his mosquito net.

Frazer turned on one of the electric lanterns, setting the light to the lowest level so it shed just a weak yellow glow.

'I hope Oti will be all right,' said Amazon.

Frazer did not reply. He wasn't the kind of kid

who hid his feelings well, and his inner turmoil showed on his face. He felt that he should have been the one to have risked his life like that, not a boy they hardly knew.

'I . . . I thought he was chicken,' he said eventually.

Amazon was going to reply. Then she remembered that she was carrying something in her clenched fist. She opened it and saw two things. One she almost expected: it was a foil layer of blister-packed pills. But there was something else.

'My toothbrush!' said Frazer, a smile spreading over his face.

The two of them looked at the pills and toothbrush in astonishment for a few moments.

'He must have somehow sneaked into Huru Huru's house, while we were watching through the window, and grabbed the pills and the brush. And the clever kid didn't bring the whole box, so that thug probably won't even notice that they're missing.'

'Anyone who could do that should be able to escape those goons,' said Amazon hopefully.

'But that leaves the whole question of what we do next,' said Frazer. 'Do you think they were talking about the turtles?'

'It had to be. What do they want them for? Please don't say soup, like the sharks' fins . . .'

Frazer shook his head. 'I don't think so. I reckon baby turtles are pretty valuable alive. People like cute pets . . .'

'I think we should wake Bluey up,' said Amazon, 'and give him some of this medication. He'll know what to do.'

That, however, proved trickier than they hoped. Bluey was very groggy. He opened his mouth and swallowed two of the antihistamines, but they got little sense out of him. He stared at them through filmy eyes and tried to say his thanks, but then slumped down again.

Amazon had been trying so hard to be strong, but the tension and fear of the past few days suddenly caught up with her, and she found that tears were streaming down her cheeks.

'What are we supposed to do?' she said. 'We're only kids, and those two villains, Chung and Huru Huru, are going to take all the turtles, and Bluey's still sick, and I'm worried to death about my parents, and . . . and . . .'

Frazer was happier dealing with poisonous snakes and man-eating lions than he was with frightened young girls. And the truth is he was frightened himself. But then he looked down and caught sight of the TRACKS badge on his shirt. He took Amazon's hand and made what he knew was the most important speech of his life.

'Zonnie, we're still alive and so is our mission. We've saved one batch of turtles and we're damned well going to save the rest. Bluey is the second toughest person I've ever met: I've seen him wrestle crocs and stand up to a charging rhino. This allergic reaction has laid him low, but now we've got the pills he'll soon be right as rain, as you Brits say. In the morning we'll be back up to full strength, and together we're a match for one bloated chief and one mad animal smuggler – if that's what Chung is.'

Amazon knew that Frazer was partly faking it. But she also knew that true courage comes not from feeling no fear, but from overcoming it, and that's what Frazer was doing. And if he could then she could. She squeezed his hand back.

'Fraze,' she said, a half-smile on her lips.

'Yep?'

'You said Bluey was the second toughest person you've met . . .?'

'Yeah?'

'So who's the first?'

'Well, I'm naming no names, but she's stood up to killer squid, deadly sharks and, back in Siberia, leopards, bears and tigers. And I once shot her in the butt with a tranquillizer dart and she hardly complained.'

'I was asleep,' she said, now grinning. 'Or, believe me, I'd have complained! But now,' she added, yawning, 'sleep seems like a good idea. You're right, tomorrow things will be . . . better.'

30

Crime and Punishment

The next morning things did indeed, for a while at least, seem to be better. Bluey was greatly improved. He was still weak, and his legs were like jelly, but his mind at least was clear, and he gulped down two more of the pills with a glug of water.

'I was a fool to trust Chung,' he said bitterly, after Frazer and Amazon had updated him on the situation. 'As you guessed, he's plainly after the turtles. Probably for the pet trade. Well, we're gonna make sure he doesn't get them. The key here is the sat phone. It's obvious now that it's being blocked from the *Tian-long*. We have to try it from the other side of the island. Or even take a canoe out beyond the lagoon. In the meantime we –'

He stopped and looked at Frazer, who was in the doorway.

'Sorry, Frazer, am I boring you? Because, you know, this is pretty important stuff.'

'Sorry, Bluey, it's the sky. I don't like the look of it

up there. The clouds seem even angrier and the air is as heavy as Huru Huru.'

Amazon joined him in some sky-gazing, and then more earthly matters caught her eye. 'And *I* don't like the look of what's going on over there,' she said, pointing down the beach towards the village.

A crowd was gathering by the beach in front of the huts. At the heart of the throng was the huge figure of Huru Huru, and with him was Oti, looking as fragile as a butterfly about to be trampled by an elephant. The other villagers formed a half-circle round them.

Frazer turned to his cousin. 'I owe him one. It's all my fault. I've a feeling this isn't to do with the medicine – it's that wretched toothbrush. Follow me in a minute, with Bluey. He speaks some Polynesian – he may be able to explain what has happened to the villagers and get them on our side – but he'll need your help walking over there. I'm going to go and make this right.'

Then Frazer dived quickly into the hut, grabbed the toothbrush and pelted along the beach towards the crowd.

Amazon began to follow him for a few steps, then paused, thought and decided that Frazer for once was right. But an idea also began to form in the back of her mind. She went back to the hut.

It took Frazer thirty seconds flat out to reach the scene on the beach. By the time he got there, things had taken a grim turn. Oti was on his knees, firmly held by the grinning Moipu. Huru Huru was towering over the boy. And the enormous chief was carrying that terrifying war club in his huge hand. He waddled round the kneeling boy, declaiming clamorously in his own tongue. But it didn't take a skilled linguist to work out that what he was saying was very bad news for Oti. And one word came out loud and clear in English – 'Toothbrush!'

One man stepped forward and said something quietly to Huru Huru. Begging for mercy on behalf of the child, Frazer thought. The chief stopped pacing, glared briefly and then delivered a vicious backhanded slap to the villager, the blow landing with the sound of a spade hitting a ripe peach. It sent him spinning back on to the ground.

Huru Huru then issued a command, and Moipu took the boy's arm and stretched it out. Huru Huru raised the mighty club above his head.

Frazer watched from outside the circle, fascinated, horrified, frozen.

No, not frozen.

He pushed through the circle and screamed, 'STOP!'

Huru Huru turned, his face puzzled, then amused. Oti looked at Frazer and shook his head, and silently mouthed, 'Run!' But Frazer wasn't running. He'd had enough of that last night.

'You, little boy?' boomed the chief. 'I told you to

162

keep out of the affairs of *my* village. This is none of your business. Go back to your turtles while you are still able.'

'This *is* my business.' Frazer held the bright red toothbrush out towards Huru Huru, almost as if it were a weapon. 'And this is my toothbrush. I took it back from you. It's got nothing to do with this kid.'

Huru Huru looked at the toothbrush, and then at Frazer, and then back at the brush. And then, to Frazer's great surprise, the big man began to laugh. But this was not a laugh of good humour. It was a huge, rolling laugh that was also a shout, and a sneer, and a threat.

Moipu joined in with the laughter, and stony-faced Tipua made a noise like heavy rocks being ground together, which may also have been his attempt at mirth.

'I see now,' said Huru Huru, once the waves of laughter had died down. 'I thought that the boy here –' he pointed a sausage finger at Oti – 'had been acting alone. Now I see that he was enticed and corrupted by you. This is what happens when the simplicity and innocence of my people is infected by the evil ways of you outsiders, with your bribes, promises and lies.'

Huru Huru then translated his own words for the villagers, as his brothers grunted and goaded. The crowd murmured a little, but still did not raise their eyes from the ground.

All through Huru Huru's speech, Frazer had been getting madder and madder. It wasn't just that the chief was a bully, although Frazer hated bullies more than any other kind of human being. It was that he was a fraud.

'I think you're a phoney,' said Frazer. And then he remembered the word he'd been searching for, the one that meant something like phoney and fake and liar all mixed up together. 'A phoney and a *hypocrite*. You don't care about these people. You only care about yourself and your fat belly. These guys all live in poverty, while you live in your palace. And all that money you've got in your Swiss bank account – don't tell me it's for the villagers. It's so you can go on living in luxury. I know there aren't any real cannibals any more in Polynesia, but in a way you *are* a cannibal – you're eating your own people alive.'

Frazer wasn't just saying this because it was true. He also had a plan. Well, plan was putting it a bit strongly. It was more of an idea. Probably a bad one, but, he'd always believed, a bad idea is better than no idea at all. Well, usually.

His idea was to enrage Huru Huru, to make him act rashly, to force him to swing that heavy club of his. Frazer had been learning martial arts ever since he could walk. He was pretty good at tae kwon do and karate, which were both all about rapid-fire kicks and punches, while blocking your enemy. But that wouldn't work here against a monster like Huru Huru. Punching

164

him would be like punching a building, and trying to block that war club would be like blocking a tank.

No, this was the time for aikido – an offshoot of ju-jitsu that involved using your opponent's weight and force against him. It was specifically designed for a situation like this: a strong oaf with a weapon against a weaker, unarmed but faster guy. That's why he had to get Huru Huru to swing his club. Then he would use his favourite move: *gokyo*, the so-called fifth technique. Left hand on your opponent's elbow, right hand on his wrist, a pivot, a turn and your enemy would be on the floor, and his weapon was yours.

Frazer was convinced that, as soon as the villagers saw their chief humiliated by a mere kid, they would turn on him and his dumb brothers, and cast them all out of the village and off the island. They'd be free and he'd be the hero. Hey, maybe they'd make up cool songs about him. There was a fighting chance that they'd worship him as a god, and in hundreds of years' time they'd still be talking about Frazalua (or whatever), the young warrior who had saved them all from the evil demon Huru Bigbutt . . .

But first the chief had to swing. Frazer was already on the balls of his feet, waiting to move.

31

Machete!

He never got the chance. The mistake that Frazer made was a common one: to assume that because Huru Huru was a bully he must also be stupid. Life would be a lot easier if bullies were always stupid. His brothers may have been stupid, but Huru Huru was not.

'I see that you are not without courage, boy,' he said. 'But courage is a toothless shark when there is no brain.'

Distracted by the looming presence of his adversary, Frazer failed to sense that Tipua had come up behind him. He now seized Frazer's upper arms with a grip like an eagle's talons.

Huru Huru came very close to Frazer's face, so close that he could see the fibres of grey meat stuck in between his brown teeth, smell his breath like some thick concentrate of all the world's rottenness, feel the moist heat pulsing from his swollen body. Frazer thought he was going to be sick, but somehow fought it down, although he could not fight his body's overwhelming urge to pull away.

Huru Huru sensed his revulsion and savoured it, the way you might relish an ice cream, or a good book. His smile widened into a grin, and then was replaced by a look of fake concern.

'Now, truly, I was only going to give your friend here a little bruise – something he could brag about to the younger children. It would let him play the hero. "Look how brave I am, standing up to Huru Huru the ogre!" he would say. But now I am going to do something a little more . . . let me see . . . *dramatic*. Something a little more permanent.'

And then Huru Huru put out his hand to Tipua, and, with a sound not entirely unlike *shwiiinnngg*, a machete was drawn from a sheath.

'But that's . . . that's mine!' said Frazer, and he knew that his voice sounded petulant and silly.

So much for Frazalua the hero.

'Yes, it is yours. And I trust you will appreciate the . . . what is the word . . .? Yes, the *irony*. You see, it is because of you that I do this. I want you to remember this – the thing that I shall now do – for the rest of your life. I want you to think about it as you fall asleep. I want it to stalk your nightmares. I want it to be there with you when you wake up in the morning. I want it to hum in your mind as you *he he he* brush your teeth.'

And then Huru Huru came close again to Frazer,

closer even than before, and he spoke quietly, confidingly, in his ear.

'Do you know what the best part of the human body is to eat, hmmm? According to the old ones that is, the ones that taught me, the ones who kept true to the old ways. Shall I tell you, hmmm? Not the fleshy parts, no. Not the leg or the breast, like a chicken, or the belly, like a pig. Oh no. It is the hand, roasted slowly and picked clean, with your teeth.'

And then, with that surprising speed that seemed a product of some supernatural force of evil within the man, Huru Huru spun round, raised the machete and brought it whistling through the air towards Oti's thin wrist.

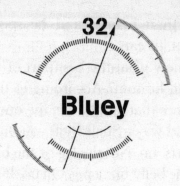

32

Bluey

Before the machete had completed its grisly downward journey, a blur burst through the circle of watchers and cannoned into Huru Huru.

'Bluey!' Frazer exclaimed, a grin lighting up his face.

Yes, his friend was here and everything would be OK now.

He looked around for Amazon. Where was she? Surely she hadn't left Bluey to stagger here all by himself? But there wasn't time to think about it. It turned out that 'burst' couldn't have been a more inappropriate verb for Bluey's actions. It was probably intended as a rugby tackle, but the young Aussie could only stutter and lurch towards the Polynesian man-mountain.

Huru Huru didn't even bother to fend him off. He just let him rebound off his colossal torso, the way you sometimes see a moth bounce off a lampshade. Bluey, who, with his ghostly white flesh and black-circled eyes, looked like a skeleton, staggered back to his feet and made another rush at Huru Huru. Seemingly enjoying himself, this time the chief actively thrust his huge stomach at Bluey, propelling him metres across the sand.

Moipu and Tipua guffawed. Someone from the crowd – an old man who had, Frazer thought, nothing to lose – went to try to help Bluey, but Moipu first thrust Oti aside, and then kicked the old man to the ground. He unhooked his own war club from the belt around his waist and brandished it at the men and women and children, daring another to step out of line.

Bluey tried to rise again and failed. He looked totally spent.

Frazer struggled vainly against the grip of Moipu. 'You big bully,' he spat, hardly even looking at Huru Huru.

For his part, the chief ignored the boy. He seemed to be thinking things over, weighing up deep issues in his mind. He mumbled something to himself. Frazer thought it might have been 'They'll never find the bodies,' or perhaps that was just his imagination running wild. And then Huru Huru shrugged his huge meaty shoulders and walked towards Bluey, who was still slumped on the white coral sand.

With horror, Frazer saw that Huru Huru was still carrying the machete and the war club. He struggled, but Tipua's hands held him tight.

'Get up, Bluey, get up!' he yelled. 'You've got to run.'

Bluey looked at him and shook his head. His eyes were watery and pale and he had nothing left to give.

Frazer twisted round to look into the eyes of the man holding him.

'Please,' he said, as much with his eyes as his mouth, trying to appeal to some flicker of humanity in the soul of Tipua. All he got for his trouble was a cuff across the head.

It was all Frazer needed. With only one hand holding him, he twisted easily out and to the side, held Tipua's wrist with his left hand and drove his right hand into his elbow. There was only one way for Tipua to go, and he collapsed on to one knee. Frazer knew that the correct aikido move would be to throw him all the way down and then back away.

But he needed to do more than just put Tipua on the floor. Saying a silent 'sorry' to the sensei who had trained him, he drove his hand into the elbow and pulled back on the wrist. There was a crunch and a scream of agony from the Polynesian. Frazer had dislocated his elbow, and the pain, he knew, would be exquisite and disabling.

He ran to Bluey and stood over his prone form.

'You . . . run . . . go . . .' he heard Bluey rasp.

'Ain't going nowhere, mate,' Frazer replied in a truly terrible Aussie accent. It got, he thought, a laugh out of Bluey. Or possibly a sob. 'The Trackers do not leave a comrade when he's down.'

Huru Huru walked slowly over to where Tipua

rolled on the floor, weeping. He spat on him, kicked sand in his face and issued some Polynesian curse. Then he looked at Frazer and shrugged.

'Can't get the staff,' he said. 'Even when you share a mother. I'm sorry, my boy, but I am going to have to kill you now. It will be quick, you have earned that.'

Then he raised the machete and the war club, and moved his bulk back towards Frazer and Bluey.

Frazer adopted his loose and easy aikido stance.

'It's not my day to die,' he said, but it was empty bravado. His heart truly quaked and his soul trembled. For a tiny fraction of a second the life ahead of him appeared, like a supernova: a flash of energy and light. The things he would achieve, the good he would do, the fun he would have. He saw a blizzard of images, surfing, climbing, flying, diving, saving animals, all with Amazon in tow.

Amazon, where was she?

It didn't matter. She couldn't help.

And he didn't want her to see how this must end.

Huru Huru paused a moment. Perhaps he was thinking about how this boy had broken Tipua's elbow. But then he licked his lips and came on, swinging the machete before him, as if he were hacking his way through the jungle.

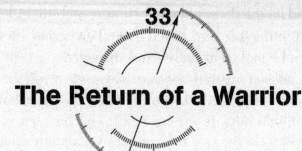

33

The Return of a Warrior

'I see that you have matched yourself against a child and a sick man: it is lucky for you that the little girl is not here also, or it would be you lying in the sand, Huru Huru.'

The chief turned towards the voice, slowly, like a mill wheel drawn by oxen. He was not smiling now, although the figure facing him was.

Joy and hope suddenly flooded into Frazer's heart.

'Matahi . . . how did you . . .?' Frazer had been going to ask how he'd got there – the last thing he'd known Matahi had been on the ship, still ill. But the water dripping from the tall man's body told him exactly how he had reached them: he had swum through the shark-infested waters.

'So,' rumbled Huru Huru, talking to the crowd, 'the vagabond returns. The scum who would not even stay for the funeral of his own father, our beloved former chief, Tuvali.'

'You know very well that if I had stayed then I

would have met with the same fate as my father. But now I am back. I am here to take you to stand trial in the French court in Tahiti. You shall know justice then for all of your crimes.'

Huru Huru laughed now, that same forced, ogreish laugh as before.

'So speaks the coward Matahi. A real man would request trial by combat. But, no, Matahi the mouse would take me to the French court, like a woman.'

'I was hoping that you would say something like this, Huru Huru. Had I merely killed you without giving you the chance to stand trial, then I would have been as bad as you. But now you have walked openly into the arms of your fate. Yes, Huru Huru, I challenge you to combat. Choose the time, choose the place, choose the weapons.'

Huru Huru's face became serious, but it seemed to Frazer like a sham.

'I choose now. I choose here. And, for my weapons, I CHOOSE THESE!'

Huru Huru brandished the machete in his left hand and the war club in his right, and charged at the unarmed Matahi, yelling out his blood-curdling war cry. Truly in that moment, with his tattoos and his face contorted with rage, Huru Huru looked like a demon summoned up from the depths of hell.

Matahi, it seemed, knew his opponent well. He was not remotely taken by surprise, but merely sidestepped the onward rush of the chief, who blundered into the circle of watchers, sending a dozen men, women and children flying.

It reminded Frazer of the time he'd watched elephant seals fighting on a beach in northern California, squashing any pups that got in their way.

Huru Huru growled. That is the only word for it. An animal sound, full of the wrath of ages. And then he gathered himself, and Frazer could see how he chained his rage, harnessed it, focused it. Yes, this was no animal, but a clever and evil human being, full of cunning and intelligence.

He began to circle round Matahi, the two men's eyes fixed on each other.

Huru Huru feinted with the club, and then slashed down with the machete, missing Matahi's shoulder by millimetres.

With the bigger man slightly off balance, Matahi took the chance to launch an attack. He aimed two quick kicks at the chief's knees, trying to bring him down, and then threw a hard punch that thudded into the side of Huru Huru's head.

Neither the kicks nor the punches appeared to have any effect.

It struck Frazer that Matahi was still weak from his injury and the infection that had followed – he could see the scabs and rawness from the rasping teeth and suckers of the squid all over the man's back and leg. He was not ready for this fight, and yet he had come . . .

'This is all you have?' Huru Huru bellowed. 'You must have been living with the women on Tahiti, for life away from our island has made you soft, like a girl. You are not even fit to be buried like a man: when I have killed you, I will just throw you to the dogs, who will feast on your soft heart.'

As it was intended to do, this goaded Matahi into a rash attack. Frazer, putting himself into the mind of Matahi, could see what he was trying. A feint with the left, expecting that Huru Huru would sway away from it, giving Matahi the chance to drive his right fist into his mouth.

But Huru Huru had fought many battles in his time, and was wise to such tricks. He ignored the feint, knowing that he could ride any punch, and then he simply swung his war club in a low arc, where it smacked into the side of Matahi's leg.

There was no way to resist the might of the blow – in fact, if Matahi had tried, his leg would have snapped in two. So he allowed the blow to sweep him off his feet. Huru Huru could have finished him off, but he chose instead to turn and roar his triumph, like a professional wrestler trying to get the crowd worked up.

And then he returned. He dropped the machete and held the war club in both hands: he was going to finish this in the old way.

Frazer had been transfixed by the battle. Now he knew he had to do something to help Matahi. He looked around for a weapon to throw to his friend, but saw nothing. Then he decided that he had to use himself as a weapon, and prepared to throw *himself* at Huru Huru to buy Matahi the time to get up.

He never got the chance.

The Sting in the Tail

When Frazer left the hut to help Oti, Amazon had rushed to Bluey's side. She spoke urgently to him, explaining her plan.

'Mad . . .' he'd mumbled, as she helped him up. But the force of her determination won him over, and he dragged himself slowly across the beach towards the grim and chaotic scene in front of the village. Amazon sped in the opposite direction.

But now she was back.

She was holding the spotted red scarf that her mother had given her before she had disappeared. It was her most cherished possession. But, as a weapon, it really didn't stack up. Then again it didn't need to: it's not the gun that kills you, but the bullet.

She darted in from the crowd, completely unseen by Huru Huru. And then, when she was a metre away, she leapt up and slapped the neckerchief against Huru Huru's neck.

He stopped and stared at her, and then put his

hand to the place that she'd struck. There was something there. Something about the size of a lady's brooch. And it was as beautiful as a brooch as well, a blue and white enamelled broach. Huru Huru touched it. It was moist. He pulled. It resisted, as if clinging to the skin of his throat. And then it peeled away and he looked at it, a puzzled expression on his face.

What he was looking at, of course, was a certain small blue mollusc, the favourite food of which was the fearsome collectivist organism, with a passing resemblance to a jellyfish.

Amazon had gone back to the place where Bluey had been stung, and then found the dead Portuguese man-of-war and its beautiful but deadly predator in the pool. The sea slug had been munching its way through the tentacles, absorbing the stinging cells, and concentrating them into a weapon of truly awesome power.

Huru Huru hurled the blue mollusc away towards the sea, but the damage had been done. The stinging cells, those little harpoons, had fired and delivered their agonizing cargo of poison into both his neck and his hand. He fell to his knees, foaming and frothing at the mouth.

Huru Huru tried to speak, but all that came out was a hoarse croaking. 'Help me . . .' And then the croak gave way to a juddering, silent scream, as the chief writhed and squirmed grotesquely on the ground.

Matahi was on his feet again by now. He limped over to Huru Huru.

Frazer looked in wonder at Amazon.

'Remind me never to get on your bad side,' he said.

'You already are,' she replied, with a pert smile.

Then they ran to Bluey and helped him up. The three of them, arm in arm, then became spectators for the next act in the drama.

Matahi was speaking to the crowd in his own language. It wasn't hard to work out what he was saying. He was the true chief, the son of the beloved Tuvali, and he was come to reclaim what was rightfully his.

And then he glanced at the Trackers and switched to English, as he addressed his fallen rival, who still squirmed on the floor in silent agony.

'Huru Huru, for what you have done, you deserve to perish. I could let you die here in torment, or I could put an end to it, and you.'

He picked up the vicious war club and weighed it in his hands, as if appreciating its heft and balance. Huru looked up at him with bloodshot eyes.

'Mercy,' he may have said, or perhaps it was some other Polynesian word, a hex or a promise.

Amazon made as if to go towards Matahi. She was going to tell him that he must be humane, that he should not stoop to the same level as Huru Huru, but Bluey put a hand on her shoulder.

'He knows what he's doing,' he said.

And then Matahi looked at Moipu and Tipua.

'Take him. Wash the sting in seawater. Then take a canoe to the big ship and leave this island forever. Your friend Chung will take care of you. Or perhaps just throw you to the sharks. I do not care.'

The two men looked sickeningly grateful to have escaped with their lives. They did as they were bidden and, ten minutes later, they were paddling a large twin-hulled canoe towards the gap in the reef, with Huru Huru lying on the platform between the two hulls, as the villagers hurled abuse (as well as some rather unpleasant material gathered from the pigpen) in their direction.

'I think,' said Bluey to Matahi, 'that you owe us an explanation.'

The noble Polynesian smiled and nodded.

'All good stories must be accompanied by a feast.'

'Now you're talking!' said Frazer.

'Not quite yet,' said Bluey, who had dragged himself up on to his feet. 'We've still got our mission. Chung is still on the loose and he wants those turtles.'

Matahi grasped his arm. 'You are right, my friend. But now that my people have been freed from the tyranny of Huru Huru, Chung has no allies on this island. During my time on the ship I learned much about this man. He sails the seas finding rare animals to sell to America. Parrots, Komodo dragons and turtles. But he is a wicked businessman and not a warrior. He has many of our pearls, and will not have to pay for them now that Huru Huru is no more. I believe that he will go to another place where his evil is not so well known.

'My people were crushed, but now they are free, and they will help you with your great task. I will set men to watch the beaches, and together we will carry the little ones into the water, if there is a need. Tomorrow there is much work to do, but now it is our way to celebrate a victory, and I promise you a Polynesian feast is not something that you will ever forget.'

35

Party Poopers

The feast was, indeed, mighty. It was eaten on the beach, around a huge fire of driftwood, with the setting sun as a backdrop. For, amazingly, the clouds had lifted, and for only the second time on their Polynesian adventure, the world looked to Amazon as she felt it was supposed to: beautiful blues and greens, melting into the gold.

And, once the sun had set, out came the astounding stars, and then a moon so bright it almost hurt the eyes to stare at it. Even the *no-nos* were kept at bay by the smoke from the fire.

They were served fish and pork that had been wrapped in banana leaves and baked under the ground in an earth oven. There were great piles of gaudily coloured fruit, and bowls of the thick porridge called *poi*, made from mashed-up taro roots.

Bluey, fortified by the allergy medication, was feeling much better, and he and Frazer tucked into everything with great gusto.

At last Amazon and Frazer found themselves in the midst of Polynesian culture at its vibrant, noisy, exuberant best. The men and women took it in turns to dance, while the children copied their steps, and fell over their feet. The men's dancing was full of martial vigour, with comical facial grimaces and lunges with imaginary spears. The women dancers were more elegant, forming lines of swaying hips and undulating arms.

The singing was extraordinary, by turns low and percussive and high and melodic. Among many unfamiliar but haunting melodies, Amazon recognized some old hymns that she had sung at school, but they were warped and twisted and taken into new and thrilling directions.

Matahi translated the words of the songs for them. Some were tales of tragic love. Others were stories of the old gods, filled with drama and darkness. Another told of the great sea voyages from a thousand years ago, setting out into the unknown and finding new lands at the rim of the world.

The men of the village passed round wooden bowls of kava.

Matahi offered it to Bluey, who took a long drink. Then it was Frazer's turn.

'Just a sip,' said Bluey, 'so you can tell people you've tried it.'

'What is this stuff?' Frazer asked, sniffing it suspiciously.

'It's made from the root of the kava plant, a member of the pepper family. The women chew it up and spit out the pulp. That gets mixed with water, left to stew for a while, then you drink it. It makes your tongue go numb, and then you fall asleep.'

'Thanks,' said Frazer. 'But I think I'll give it a miss.'

It was time, at last, for Matahi's story. The whole village gathered round to listen, even though most of them would only understand fragments and scraps.

'My father, Tuvali, was a great man. He sailed all over the Pacific, sometimes with your fathers, who called him by the name Omo. This you know. What you do not know is that his father, Oto, was the chief of this village. Oto was a strong man and a fierce warrior, and Tuvali argued with him, and left the island. Finally he heard word that his father was dying and came home. He was reconciled with his father, and was at his side as he died. Then for many years my father was the chief. But he was a different sort of chief to Oto. He was a kind man, as well as a strong one. He said that the men and women of the village must make decisions together. He said that all people were equal, that there should not be chiefs and lesser men.

'And my father taught the village the way of farming the black pearls, which he had learned of in his wanderings. It was a way of earning the village money without harming the ocean or the land. The money would buy things for the village. Clean water and sanitation. Materials for the huts. He wanted to build a school for the children. In fact, the school building was begun – it is now the house of Huru Huru, that you have seen.

'But not all of the people of the village agreed with my father. Huru Huru said that my father was a coward. He even sometimes said that my father was not the same Tuvali who had left the village, but an impostor.

'My father should have banished Huru Huru, but it was not his way. He tried to make Huru Huru understand that he was wrong. And Huru Huru pretended to change. But all the time he was plotting with his brothers Moipu and Tipua. They even pretended to be *my* friend. And as my mother was dead and I had no brothers or sisters that made my heart glad.

'And then, one black night, they came into my father's hut – the same hut where you are now staying – and they slew Tuvali as he slept. Huru Huru stove in his skull with his war club. I saw this with my own eyes. I awoke just as the blow was struck. I tried to fight them, but I was only a boy of sixteen, and they were too strong for me. I would also have been killed, but I managed to flee. I took a canoe from the beach and sailed away, my eyes blinded by my tears.

'Then began my own years of wandering, as I waited to become strong enough to defeat Huru Huru and his brothers. For many years I travelled through the islands working as a labourer or a ship hand. And then I knew it was time to return. I met the boy Oti, who was returning to the island after his time in Tonga. He told me of the tyranny of Huru Huru. He told me that he sold the island's pearls to a wicked trader from the Philippines.

'I sought this man on the Marquesas, and planned to return to the island on his ship. It was the day before we sailed that I also learned that the children of my father's old friends were also trying to get to the island. I thought at first that this was a great coincidence, but now I know that it was fate. I took the place of your guide, that day. I did not tell you about my purpose because I knew that if the man Chung found out then he would not take me to the island.'

'I thought it was all a bit of a coincidence,' said Frazer.

'All that happens, happens for a reason,' replied Matahi. 'But I did not know that you would be able to help me as you did. I owe you my life. And my village owes you its life as well, for surely Huru Huru was bleeding it to death.

'Long ago my father and your fathers became brothers. Now I am your brother.'

And then Matahi gave them each a magnificent

black pearl and he, Amazon, Frazer and Bluey all swore lifelong friendship.

It was three very full and very happy Trackers who went to bed back in their hut late that night, as the moon hung over the lagoon and sent lines of silver light flickering over the waters.

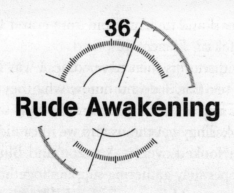

36

Rude Awakening

The rats were chasing him. Hundreds, thousands, millions. Their yellow teeth gnashed and snapped as he fled before them. They pursued him through the forest. His legs were moving so slowly, tangled up in vines and other things that clutched at him as he passed. The hands of the dead. Bony fingers. Ahead of him he saw the safety of the hut. Would he reach it in time, or would the rats catch him? He jumped, sailing through the air like a flying fish. He reached the doorway. He was inside. He turned. The rats were still coming, rushing towards him blindly. He smiled. He opened his mouth and the rats jumped in.

And now he was choking. He could not breathe. The rat was in his mouth. Panic surged like lava in his chest. He opened his eyes.

'Frazer, be silent,' hissed Matahi in the darkness. His hand was over Frazer's mouth to prevent him from crying out. He saw Amazon and Bluey moving about in the dark of the hut.

Matahi slowly took his hand from Frazer's mouth.

'What is it?' Frazer whispered.

'Chung and his men have come. I was wrong. I did not see this. I do not know why they care so much. They have the pearls. I thought that they would go. They have guns and we must hide.'

Frazer looked over at Amazon and Bluey, who were desperately gathering supplies together.

'But how . . .? It's a small island. There's nowhere to hide.'

'There are places. Secret caverns under the ground dug by our ancestors. We may be able to hide for a time, and the foreigners will grow tired and leave. But we must go now.'

Seconds later, the Trackers followed Matahi out through the door. It was just before dawn, and the sky in the east was beginning to lighten, and stars still glittered in the lagoon. Outside they met Oti, who was standing guard. The two Polynesians spoke hurriedly together.

'We must –' began Matahi when suddenly the hut was lit up with bright torches, and a gunshot shattered the silence.

'I suggest you don't move unless you want a few more holes in your skin than nature intend.'

'Chung!' exclaimed Frazer and Amazon together, and then the man himself strode forward, accompanied by a dozen members of his crew. Chung had a heavy automatic pistol, and the others had a collection of handguns, rifles and sub-machine guns.

Without hesitating, Matahi leapt at one of the men and twisted the weapon from his hands, and clubbed him to the floor.

'Come!' he yelled, but it was already too late. Shots rang out, muzzle flashes showing orange in the darkness. Matahi had no choice but to turn and run, with Oti at his heels. Chung coughed out orders and three men set off after them.

Amazon was going to follow Matahi, but Bluey put his hand on her shoulder.

'Let him go. He has a chance without us. And I don't believe Chung will do us any harm. He has no quarrel with us. And I have to put your safety first.'

'Very wise, Mr Blue,' said Chung. 'If you misbehave or try any heroics, then I have to shoot one of children. Maybe just in leg. Maybe in guts and you watch die slowly in front of you. Also, you very wrong about something. Chung has small quarrel with you. OK, maybe not quarrel, but a slight, ah, shall we say difference of opinion. You see, you want to make little baby turtle safe by helping them across sand and into sea. I think best to help baby turtle in different way. I think polite to take them away from this dangerous island and these seas, all full of shark, squid, barracuda and other hungry creatures that want to gobble them up. Chung think best to sell them to rich Americans who look after very nice, make turtle happy, make Chung happy.'

'I knew it!' exclaimed Amazon. 'It's the turtles. You were always after them.'

'And the sat phone,' Frazer chipped in. 'You've been jamming it, haven't you? That's why I couldn't get through to my dad . . .'

'Oh, sure, my little boat has got all mod cons. And, yes, girl, that is Chung's job. Pearls are just hobby. My main business is animal import-export. Baby turtle fetch a thousand dollar in US. On these beaches there are maybe ten thousand turtles. You do math. Don't have to, Chung do it for you. Is million dollars. I take baby turtles to Mexico. Got good friend in coastguard there. And, by Chung's calculation, today is day when turtle hatch out. And best of all is that you get to help! I got special storage boxes for turtles. Little English girl and little American boy, you please show Chung's men where is turtle nests, then run around like crazy putting turtles nice and safe in box, then Chung say farewell and leave you here on island. No hard feelings, everyone friendly, eh, yes?'

'We'll never help you, Chung – why should we?' said Frazer, his voice burning with hatred and contempt.

'Hah! Good to see boy with grit. But foolish too. This is why China and east is easily take over world – Americans is too dumb. Where was I? Oh yes, unless you do this for Chung, your friend Bluey is in for a bad time with sharks, if you get Chung's meaning. And, if you don't, I mean we feed him to sharks, which to be honest is waste of perfectly good Australian. Also should say that your old friend Huru Huru is back. But he is not same jolly fellow he was before he got tickled with that pretty slug. Between you and Chung, he a bit loco-loco . . .' Chung twiddled his finger at the side of his head in the universal sign for crazy.

'I don't like that guy. He too greedy, also deep down not nice. He likes to make other people unhappy. Not like Chung. I like everyone happy. But what I'm saying is maybe I can protect everyone from Huru Huru, if everyone helps Chung with little problem of how to collect all those baby turtle. You understand?'

Without waiting for an answer, Chung dropped his comical, almost friendly tone and barked out more orders, and three burly men came forward and grabbed Bluey. Frazer saw his Australian friend battle within himself, fighting his natural urge to get a punch or two in before they overpowered him. But, as he'd said, his prime responsibility was the two children, and so he allowed himself to be bound without a struggle.

'Do as he tells you,' he said as they led him away. 'There'll be another day when things pan out differently.'

37

The New Queen of Uva'avu

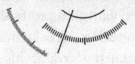

What followed was a morning that was both miraculous and terrible.

Chung assigned Frazer to the village beach, while Amazon was sent to the turtle beach. Each had two minders who kept them covered with their guns. Each beach had three large boxes, designed to contain the newly hatched turtles, keeping them safe and secure.

Bluey was tied to a palm tree by the Trackers' hut. A bored guard watched over him, smoking cigarette after cigarette, while yet more of the crew scoured the island looking for Matahi and Oti.

From his part of the beach, Frazer could see into the village, and there he beheld a very strange sight indeed. The villagers lurked in their huts, intimidated by the guns, and terrified by the return of the vengeful Huru Huru.

Huru Huru, however, as Chung had indicated, was not the man he had been two days before. The second-hand stings of the sea slug had left him bloated and his skin covered in ugly red blotches.

But that was not the main change. Some combination of the terrible pain caused by the sting and the powerful toxin it contained had affected his brain in a most peculiar manner. He commanded that his enormous wooden chair – a throne in all but name – be brought down from his house to the beach in front of the village. He sat dressed not in his usual garb, but draped in elaborately decorated fabrics that Frazer strongly suspected were curtains. He had also placed on his head a brightly coloured object made from china. It took Frazer a few moments to realize that this was a chamber pot – another pointless object hoarded by Huru Huru in his greed. The comically monarchical picture was completed by the sceptre which Huru Huru carried. Not the war club that the chief had once wielded, but a folded-up pink parasol with a pretty white fringe.

And Huru Huru was not quietly regal. He was crying out in a high-pitched voice.

'I am your queen, Her Royal Highness Hura Hura. Come bow before me and offer your veneration, and I may save you from the coming maelstrom, from the catastrophe, from the end of the world.'

Huru Huru's brothers stood on either side of the throne, looking decidedly uncomfortable. And, as Huru Huru or rather Queen Hura Hura's diatribe continued, more of the villagers began to stare out of their huts, at first with fear, and then amazement, and then amusement, and finally hilarity.

But Frazer was not able to enjoy the spectacle of Huru Huru's insanity for long. All along the beach he began to notice the sand start to stir.

38

Amazon's Beach

It was already hot, even at 7 a.m. Weirdly hot. It wasn't just that Amazon had got used to the glowering skies and rain squalls. This was a strange sort of heat that seemed to press down on her skull as if she were wearing a hat made of lead.

The heavy heat and the frantic exercise made her sweat, and the sweat mingled with the tears on her face. This was all a vicious parody of the entrancing day she and Frazer had helped the first clutch of turtles to make their way to the sea. Then there was only one nest to concentrate on. Now there were dozens, all along the beach.

She was racing across the sand, scooping up the tiny turtles – hardly bigger than bottle tops – and racing with them back to the boxes, where each had its own little compartment. She had already filled two of the boxes, which contained five hundred compartments each, arranged in ten layers of fifty compartments.

In fact, the turtles were digging their way out of the buried nests at such a rate that the two guards assigned to watch over her were helping out.

Even so, a few of the little turtles managed to waddle and flap their way down as far as the water. Sadly, even more of them were snatched up by the frigate birds that had flocked to the beach, or grabbed by the countless crabs that emerged from the lagoon.

Exhausted and heartbroken as she was, Amazon could not stop. The thought of what would happen to Bluey if she and Frazer did not fill up the boxes bit and nagged at her like an attacking frigate bird. And so she ran and wept and sweated, and, helped by the two guards, the three boxes were finally filled with the tiny, vulnerable and very expensive little turtles.

As she laboured, she had gradually become aware of something strange out on the horizon. She didn't have the time to stop and look properly until the boxes were filled and the beach empty. Then she noticed that the two crew members were also staring out to sea, beyond the line of surf breaking on the reef.

Amazon shaded her eyes with her hand and followed their gaze. It looked like a solid bank of cloud so utterly black it appeared to be a slice of the night that had torn free and invaded the day. Here and there Amazon saw an intense yellow flicker.

Lightning?

'What is that?' she asked the crew, although she knew that they spoke no English. She tried in Mandarin, pointing at the black void in the distance.

They did not answer, but picked up a box each and hurried away, leaving one for Amazon. She toyed briefly with the idea of taking it straight to the water's edge and releasing the little captives, but then she thought of Bluey handcuffed to the tree. She wiped her face with her sleeve, picked up the box and, staggering under the weight, followed.

39

Hurried Departures

The scene on the village beach was utterly chaotic. Chung's men were dashing hither and thither, their leader barking orders and gesticulating wildly. The schooner, *Tian-long*, had come round to this side of the island and lay outside the reef, rolling in the heavy sea. The launch and another small boat – an inflatable – were pulled up on the beach. The crew were loading the boxes into the launch. Amazon guessed the other boat was to carry the crew back to the schooner.

But it wasn't just the crew of the *Tian-long* who were frantically busy. The villagers were also furiously active. Many were carrying bundles of possessions – cooking pots, sleeping mats, bawling babies. One small boy carried a basket full of puppies. Other villagers were dragging pigs. They were all heading out of the village, towards the slightly higher ground, where Huru Huru's house had been built.

It filled Amazon with unease. She tried to ask a

woman who was passing what was going on. The woman pointed out to sea and said something, but then hurried away, taking her two small children with her.

Amazon looked out to sea again. The threatening line of darkness was closer now. She knew it was a storm. A big one. Then she noticed something very strange. Although big waves were hitting the reef and sending great plumes of white spray over into the lagoon, there did not seem to be any wind. Could you get waves without wind? The evidence was here right before her eyes, but it seemed to defy logic.

At least the crew were too busy to be bothered with her. She ran over to Frazer, who was squatting by Bluey, still handcuffed to the tree.

'I can't believe this is happening,' said Frazer, shaking his head. 'Total and utter failure. That psychotic crook is going to get away with almost every turtle on this island, and there's not a darn thing we can do about it. I'd like to spit in his eye. And then spit in his other eye. And if he had more eyes I'd keep on spitting until . . . well, anyway . . .'

'I know how you feel,' said Bluey. 'But I'm not sure that's the worst of our troubles. Have you seen what's coming?'

'You mean the storm?' said Amazon. 'Yeah, looks really bad. And the villagers are all heading out.'

'It's way worse than bad,' said Bluey. 'We're in serious, serious trouble.'

By now the launch was loaded with the turtle boxes, and most of the crew were in the inflatable. Leopold Chung marched quickly up to the group of Trackers.

'OK, we all done here. Good doing business with you. All very satisfactory. I think best you go with people of village up to high ground. I think they are all try to get on roof of big house. You go too. This storm is going to be a beauty. I wish I could find place for you all on my ship, but –' Chung shrugged. 'Actually I don't want to. Bye-bye.'

'Chung, wait,' said Bluey. 'The keys, the keys for the cuffs.'

'Oh, Mr Chung not idiot. You might do something foolish, and then I have to shoot you. I throw key from boat when we out in lagoon. You got plenty time.'

And then Chung ran down to the launch. Halfway there, suddenly, and with almost no warning, a gust of wind came and knocked him completely off his feet. At the same moment a sheet of spray from the reef whipped across the lagoon and smacked into all their faces.

The inflatable was already bouncing in the swell across the lagoon, and the sudden gust lifted it clean out of the water, and the Trackers heard a wail of fear from the crew, mingled with the buzzing of the outboard motor. Miraculously, the wind set them down again the right way up, and the boat zipped on towards the schooner and safety.

Back on the beach, Chung picked himself up, looked around to see who had noticed his indignity and scuttled to the launch. There was only room for two of the crew with him, so laden was it with the boxes. The three of them – Chung was obviously worried enough about the coming typhoon to lend a helping hand – pushed the launch into the lagoon and jumped in after it. It was dangerously overloaded, and Chung had to sit on top of one of the boxes.

Frazer ran down the beach towards the launch.

'Mr Chung,' he yelled, 'the key! Don't forget the key!'

Chung made a dumbshow of checking his pockets. Then he smiled and shrugged.

'Ah, sorry, must have left on schooner. Very sorry. Easy fix – just chop down tree.'

Frazer was about to yell something appropriately rude to Chung, but he didn't get the chance. A scream came from behind him. He turned and beheld the extraordinary sight of Huru Huru charging towards him, his regal outfit floating behind him in the freshening gale.

For a moment Frazer thought that the deranged former chief was coming to wreak his revenge for the indignities of yesterday; but then he realized that Huru Huru was staring beyond him to the sea and the launch. One of the crew members was trying to get the engine to start, but it was spluttering and coughing like a drowning man.

Huru Huru would have run right over Frazer had he not dived aside. Now the titanic Polynesian was thundering through the water. Chung finally noticed him and started to yell at the crew. At last the engine caught and the launch began to surge away. With a final effort, Huru Huru hurled himself through the air. He seemed to soar for a moment, like a Zeppelin.

'So an elephant *can* fly,' said Frazer to himself.

And then Huru Huru bellyflopped into the water, sending a wave across the bow of the launch. He was just short of the boat, but he managed somehow to thrust out a hand and grabbed the gunwale.

The launch now laboured through the water, dragging Huru Huru along. Chung pulled out his pistol and tried to fire at Huru Huru, but either his weapon was empty or jammed. Then he began to hammer with the gun at the fat fingers clutching the edge of the boat. But Huru Huru was not letting go. The launch steered for the gap in the reef, but more and more water was flowing over the gunwales and into the boat. And, as they approached the reef gap, the current surging through added another element of instability.

But all that was dwarfed by what was happening in the sky. The huge area of intense blackness was now engulfing the island. Rain began to hammer down. Except that 'down' was out by exactly ninety degrees. For that first gust was nothing but an emissary of what now reached them. The wind was a manic force, a demon, a monster, raging across the lagoon. It mixed up the rain and the spray and flung it in the faces of the three Trackers, who were now the only people left on the beach.

Frazer turned away from the bizarre and almost comical spectacle out on the lagoon and ran back to Amazon and Bluey – although, with the wind behind him, he felt more like a kite screaming through the air than a running boy.

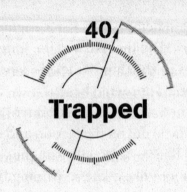

40

Trapped

'I guess we'll just have to tough it out here,' said, or rather yelled, Frazer when he reached them. The wind was now so loud only a yell could get through. The wind was tossing the tops of the palm trees around. It reminded Amazon of the hairdryer fights they'd sometimes had in the dorm back in school, with the girls trying to blast each other's hair into the weirdest shapes. 'When it blows over, we'll find a way of getting these stupid cuffs off.'

'I'm cold,' said Bluey, although Amazon and Frazer had to work it out by lip-reading. He was still weak from the allergic reaction to the Portuguese man-of-war sting, and he hadn't taken one of the pills for several hours. The three of them were in T-shirts and shorts, which had been fine for the morning weather, but now, with the rain and the wind, the temperature had dropped right down and they were all shivering.

'I'm going to get your jacket,' shouted Frazer. 'And

waterproof clothes for us too. Back in a sec. Amazon, you stay here with him. Try to keep him warm.'

Without waiting for a reply, Frazer set off, keeping as low as he could to avoid being blown over.

Amazon put her arm round Bluey. His flesh was cold.

'Need to sleep,' he said, his head nodding.

Something told Amazon that that was a bad idea.

'Stay with us, Bluey. You've got to focus. Things are going to be . . .'

And then Amazon saw what was coming: a wave that washed clean over the reef, and continued travelling relentlessly across the lagoon.

This wasn't a tsunami, which is always the result of an underwater earthquake. This was just a wall of water being driven by the wind. It reached the beach and rolled towards them, gradually losing momentum. By the time it reached them, some twenty metres from the water's edge, it had lost its force. It still swept round their feet, and on into the forest, before rolling back again and sinking into the coral sand.

For the first time Amazon began to feel real fear. She had always loved storms, and thrilled when lightning flashes had made the other girls in her dorm scream. But there was something about an English storm that was, well, safe. But this did not feel safe at all.

Her thoughts were interrupted by Frazer, who slid

next to her, gasping. He was wearing garish yellow waterproof outer-clothing, and had brought the same for Amazon and Bluey.

'That wave,' he yelled over the wind. 'It came right over the beach. I hope . . .'

'WHY ARE YOU STILL HERE?' boomed a voice, startling them all. 'YOU WILL DIE!'

41

Strange Fruit

Frazer and Amazon turned to see Matahi leaning into the storm. Then Matahi saw the handcuffs and the almost unconscious Bluey.

'These people are animals,' he said.

'Why will we die?' asked Amazon, her voice shrill with terror. 'It's only a storm . . .'

'Not any storm, the tropical cyclone, a typhoon. It will send waves right over the island. Waves that will reach halfway up this tree. All of the ground of the island will be underwater.'

Amazon and Frazer stared at each other, their mouths open.

'How long?' said Frazer, when he'd recovered from the shock.

'Minutes.'

'Can you cut this tree down, so Bluey can at least get to the higher ground?'

'Not in time. If I had known . . . I was hiding from the men with guns. I was going to return in the night.

But there is a way. Your friend must climb into the tree. We will help.'

'We?'

'Yes, me, you –'

'And Oti!' said Oti, suddenly appearing beside Matahi.

Oti went first, climbing up the tree as easily as a squirrel. The technique looked very simple. He hooked his hands round the tree, put one foot flat against the trunk and simply walked up.

Frazer and Amazon did their best to revive Bluey, but he was groggy with fatigue and illness. Matahi slid him up the trunk, and then propped him on his shoulders. Oti from above, and Frazer and Amazon from below, held him tightly there while Matahi climbed up, to begin the process again. In a way it helped that Bluey's hands were bound around the palm tree trunk – it held him fast in those moments when no one else had a good grip.

Amazon was afraid of heights, but she was also, strangely, a brilliant tree climber. She tried to follow Matahi up the palm, but she could not grip the trunk.

'Use your belt,' said Matahi, from above. 'Put it round the tree, and then use your feet, like Oti.'

Amazon didn't quite get it at first. But then she looped her belt round the trunk, slid it up until it was level with her waist, then started to walk up the tree, moving the belt with her. She wasn't sure if she was actually much use, but between the three of them, they managed to pull and push Bluey up into the relative safety of the network of branches at the top.

It was exhausting and dangerous work. The wind was growing stronger by the second, and the mix of blown spray and driving rain was blinding, deafening and painful. Now it was not only the tops of the trees that were being tossed around: the whole trunk was bending, almost like grass in a stiff English breeze.

'We will stay with your friend here,' Matahi yelled above the growing tempest. 'But there is not enough room for all of us. You and Frazer must climb that tree. Tie yourself on with your belts. Do not let go of the tree whatever happens.'

Amazon shinned down the curving trunk of the coconut palm and explained to Frazer what they must do. The tree Matahi had directed them to was taller and straighter than the one they had wrestled Bluey into, so it was a tougher climb. The trick with the belts helped, however, and in ten minutes they were both clinging to the thick palm fronds at the top of the tree, like very strange coconuts indeed.

The Tempest Rages

From their vantage point they had a view both of the other tree, with Matahi and Oti and Bluey, and across the lagoon and out to sea. The *Tian-long*, its engine straining, was desperately trying to work itself away from the reef on to which the gale was blowing it.

'Look!' said Frazer, pointing.

For a moment Amazon couldn't see what it was that her cousin was pointing at. And then she spotted it. Boxes. White boxes, floating in the water. And there was the upturned hull of the launch. Most – if not all – of the lids of the boxes had come open. There was no sign of the occupants.

'Do you think the baby turtles are OK?' asked Amazon.

'I can't tell,' replied Frazer. 'But I think so, yeah. It looks to me like either Chung opened them up so they could escape; or maybe they just came open in the wreck. Either way, I think they're free.'

'I don't see any people . . .'

'Maybe the other boat picked them up . . .?'

Amazon hated Chung and Huru Huru, but she didn't like to think of anyone out there in that deadly ocean in this storm.

Frazer shouted something else to her, but now the wind and driving rain were so bad that she just couldn't hear what it was. Then she saw that Frazer had the sat phone in his hand.

Of course! Now that the schooner was leaving, it couldn't jam their signal any more.

Frazer held on tightly with one hand, and dialled with the other. He'd almost completed his father's number when the strongest gust yet shook the tree, bending it almost down to the sand. Amazon screamed, and so did Frazer, although he'd deny it to his dying day. As the tree sprang back, he lost his grip – the rubberized surface of the phone was slick with the rain and spray. It flew from his hand, and curved in a perfect arc, heading towards the floodwater, which was by now right beneath them.

The handset was water-resistant, but it could not survive total immersion in the saltwater. Luckily, the wristband caught and tangled in the fronds at the end of the last branch, and dangled out there, beyond Frazer's reach.

Frazer was a headstrong and impetuous kid, but even he realized that it was folly to try to climb out to get the phone. They'd just have to hope it managed to hang on in there until the storm abated.

Right now abating was the very last thing on the cyclone's mind. So far, Amazon and Frazer had only seen the warm-up act. The main show was just about to begin.

Had they been able to look down from space, they would have seen a huge spiral of cloud, many hundreds of miles across, with a circle of calm at its core – the eye. The eye was an area of low pressure that sucked in the surrounding air, the way a plughole sucks in water. The eye had passed over the island that morning, and now they were in the thickest layer of insanely circling cloud mass – the part known as the eyewall. In total, the storm had as much energy in it as ten thousand nuclear warheads.

But it didn't feel like some dumb explosion to Amazon and Frazer. It felt like a living thing. An evil living thing. An evil living thing that wanted to kill them. Its huge hands took hold of their tree and shook it like a vast, malevolent baby with a rattle. If they hadn't been held tightly with their belts, the children would have been thrown out of the tree and hurled into the seething floodwaters.

Amazon looked over to Frazer, hoping to find some reassurance there. But Frazer did not look back at her. His eyes, circled black with exhaustion, wide with terror, were staring out at the lagoon. The shallow water was thrashing about, as if those same mighty hands were splashing and surging through it, but it was not the water that so terrified Frazer, but the very air itself. No, not simply the air, but the monstrous hybrid of water and air. For there, skimming across the waves, was a twister: a viciously spinning tornado.

It sucked up the water from the lagoon, along with anything else in its path. Amazon saw fish in there and, yes, even a shark. Not the monstrous tiger that had so nearly dined on her a mere couple of days ago, but still, to see a shark flying through the air like that gave an indication of the power of the thing. And now the tornado crashed into the pearl-diving platform and smashed it to fragments, pulling the wooden structure apart and hurling it back over its head as it raged past.

Lightning crackled in the storm, and Amazon almost laughed at the thought that she might end up getting fried to death amid all this water.

And water was everywhere now. It was already pawing its way up the trunk of the palm. It couldn't reach all the way to the top where they were, could it? Surely Matahi wouldn't have let them stay here if it wasn't safe? But, of course, nowhere was safe, and Matahi was simply doing the best he could.

She looked over at the tree with Bluey and the Polynesians. Oti and Matahi had their arms round the Aussie. Oti saw her looking over and gave a brave thumbs-up sign. But then the wind rose again and beat the trees so viciously that Amazon had to close her eyes.

It was, perhaps, the fact that her eyes were closed that heightened her other senses, and allowed her to detect that something strange, something truly terrible, was happening to the tree that was keeping them alive.

At first she felt it as a tremor that passed through the heartwood and into her body. And then she thought that she heard a groan. The tree itself sounded . . . what was it . . .? Defeated. Yes, as if it knew that the battle it had fought was now lost.

Amazon opened her eyes and found herself staring right into Frazer's face. He had shuffled towards her, and they were close enough now to hold hands. He took hers in his and squeezed.

He mouthed something. Amazon could not hear – she would not have heard if a gun had gone off a metre from her face. But she was sure that the word was 'sorry'.

Yes, sorry. Frazer was sorry that he had led Amazon to this place, that he had put her in this danger, that he had been responsible for her . . .

Again a groan from the tree. It was bent over so far now that the children could have reached out and touched the water. Each time this had happened, the trunk had bounced back, and the rebounding had been the most dangerous part of it all, threatening to hurl them through the air like a medieval catapult hurling stones at a castle wall. But this time the tree did not spring back. The spirit of the tree was broken. It did not snap, but merely bent lower and lower, as if it were an ancient creature, stooping to drink from the water.

43

The Fragile Ark

At precisely the same moment Amazon and Frazer realized the peril they were in. They were tied to a tree that was about to topple into the water. They would be tangled in its branches and drowned for sure. They both tore at the belts that held them. Frazer got free first and helped Amazon. At that moment the torrent carried a broken canoe towards them.

Frazer pointed and yelled, 'Jump!' There was no time to think. They both leapt into the water next to the little craft, and clung to its sides. Once their weight was lost, their palm-tree refuge did manage to pull away a little from the water, but it also seemed as though the water did not want to release it, for now a huge surge came, lifting up the canoe and twisting and pulling it out and away from the beach.

As soon as they were beyond the small shelter provided by the other trees, the children felt the full force of the typhoon. It was as if they had suddenly leapt on to a moving roller coaster. The little canoe was flung across the lagoon – although by now the lagoon was merely another small part of the raging ocean. Luckily, both Amazon and Frazer managed to get in between the hull of the canoe and the outrigger. They jammed themselves against the spars and prayed: there was nothing else that they could do.

The storm surge carried them over the reef and out on to the open sea. Around them there was nothing that looked like waves: there were just huge walls of water, moving in to crush them. This was water as sheer mass; water as power; water as the stuff not of life, but of death.

But still the children clung to their fragile ark, and still the water and the wind bore them away from the island of Uva'avu.

Frazer had a pretty good idea of the local geography. In his mind's eye he saw the Paumotu chain of islands stretching across the ocean. The Disappointment Isles – of which Uva'avu was one – were at the eastern edge of the chain. If they were blown further east, then there was no land for hundreds of miles, and even then each island was so remote that they would almost certainly miss it.

No, that way meant certain death: death from exposure or drowning, or thirst. Or shark . . .

But the other way – westward – there were countless small islands, many of them close enough to Uva'avu for him to have seen them dotting the horizon, and it would be more difficult to miss one than not. But which way had they been blown? It was impossible to say, and the sun, which would have told him, was lost behind clouds so thick that not even a sledgehammer could get through, and certainly not rays of light that had travelled ninety-three million miles from a star.

And then Frazer remembered that he was wearing his TRACKS watch, with its GPS and compass function. He hit the compass button and squinted at the screen. It was hard to read as the light refracted through the raindrops, and in any case the numbers and letters kept changing, spinning, blurring. He wasn't sure if it was the little boat that was spinning or his eyes. He tried to point the watch in the direction the wind and swell were taking them. He wiped the spray from the screen, and his heart sank. ESE. East-south-east. That way there was nothing for thousands of miles, until the coast of Argentina. That way was death.

He looked at Amazon. She had not given up. Her face was determined and strong. He was proud of his cousin. She was the real deal. A Tracker.

So he held on and hoped, and slowly began to pass out from exposure.

44

Crusoes

A cacophonous roar filled his head, as if an asylum's worth of lunatics had been miniaturized and teleported between his ears. Huge grey shapes loomed, and then receded. He was frozen and burned, frozen and burned again. He couldn't breathe. He could breathe. He couldn't breathe. Ogres grabbed and twisted his body, as if trying to wring him out like a dishcloth. And then there was peace, the peace of absence and emptiness.

'Slightly bored now.'

Frazer opened his eyes – he had been dreaming.

And closed them again, dazzled by the light. He opened them a slit and realized that the light wasn't actually that dazzling. In fact, the world was rather grey.

And then the grey world was filled by a smiling face.

'Amazon . . .' Frazer croaked. 'We're alive . . . I thought we were going to . . .'

'Yeah, me too.'

'Where . . .?'

'Somewhere in the Pacific.'

'And how did we get . . .? I must have been knocked out.'

'Actually you just fell asleep. You've been snoring worse than Bluey. Scared all the frigate birds away.'

Of course Amazon was hiding her true feelings. She'd been terrified when she woke up on the beach and found Frazer next to her, unmoving. Now she quickly wiped a tear away with her torn sleeve, hoping that he hadn't seen it.

'Can you really not remember how we got here?' she said quickly. 'How that big wave left us on the beach, but then the backwash pulled us off again and we had to scrabble for our lives?'

'Sort of. Bit hazy.' Frazer rubbed his eyes, which stung with the sea salt. 'But I don't quite get how we're on solid ground. The storm . . . we were being blown all over the place. And . . . my compass . . . I thought we were going east, and there's nothing that way. We should still be floating out there.' He waved out into the empty blue.

'I think,' said Amazon, 'the key term is "cyclone", as in "circle". The wind was spiralling round all the time, and it blew us back west again.'

'It certainly blew your hair to every point of the compass,' Frazer said, smiling.

In fact, now that he knew that, for the time being at least, they were safe, he felt happier than he could ever remember feeling before. There's nothing like rubbing shoulders with death for cheering you up.

'Cheek!' said Amazon, pretending to be annoyed. 'What do you expect: it's been through a hurricane – literally! And have you seen the state of yourself?'

Frazer stood up and checked his body. Everything seemed to be there, although his T-shirt and shorts were pretty ripped up, and the yellow waterproofs had been torn away and lost somewhere out on the wide Pacific.

He was more concerned about the canoe. Luckily, it had washed up with them. It had taken a beating: the outrigger had snapped off, as had the built-up sections at the prow and the stern. But the main hull – basically a hollowed-out tree trunk – was still in one piece.

'I think we can fix this up,' he said. 'But first I need a drink. My mouth feels like a lizard crawled in there and died.'

'I've already had a quick scout, while you were sleeping,' replied Amazon. 'There are a few puddles, but the rainwater's mixed in with the seawater, so you can't drink it. Loads of these, though –' She picked up a green coconut. 'If we could get into one then we'd at least have something to eat and drink.'

Frazer stood on a fallen trunk and had a proper look around. They were on a tiny atoll – a doughnut-shaped ring of sand that enclosed a lagoon the size of a football field. The ring of coral sand and rock was no more than ten metres wide. Everywhere he looked there were blown-down palm trees, their roots reaching grotesquely out of the earth, like trolls trying to burst from underground caverns. There were scarcely a dozen of the trees left standing in the whole atoll.

Above them, the sky was still troubled, but the huge oppressiveness of the past few days had gone, and it was obvious that the horrors of the typhoon would not be returning.

'Let's have an explore,' Frazer said. 'The first rule of survival is get to know your environment.'

'It's an island. There's sand. And some trees. That's it.'

'That's to your untrained eye,' said Frazer, knowing he was dicing with death. 'I've done a lot more of this sort of thing than you. So trust me.'

Amazon shrugged, and together they explored their sandy doughnut. It would probably have been idyllic had the storm not torn the atoll to shreds. The lagoon was full of broken branches and scattered palm leaves and, more encouragingly, coconuts – some blown down from the trees on the atoll, others from further afield.

Frazer scooped one out of the lagoon. It was heavy and dense, but still floated.

'I think I know how to get into these,' he said. 'I've read about it. What you need is a . . .' He didn't finish his sentence, but went foraging amid the broken trees.

Amazon heard a yelp, and Frazer came running out again, holding a stick in his hand. Right behind him was one of the giant coconut crabs.

'I hate those things!' said Frazer. 'You'd think there'd be one island where they weren't waiting in ambush to get me.'

Despite the predicament they were in, Amazon found it hard to suppress a giggle.

'Don't be so crabby!'

'Not even a tiny bit funny,' said Frazer, but then his face crinkled and cracked, and the two of them had to hold on to each other or they'd have fallen to the sand, so hard were they laughing.

They weren't really laughing at Amazon's pretty lame joke, but rather it was the result of the pent-up terror they had felt, combined with the simple joy of being alive.

'What's the stick for?' asked Amazon when they'd regained control of themselves again.

'I'll show you.'

It was a good stout stick, which had snapped, leaving one jagged edge.

'You really need a knife or a machete to sharpen one end – but then if you had a machete you wouldn't really need the stick. Anyway, here we go.'

He drove and twisted the blunt end of the stick into the sand. Then he sat with his legs either side of it, raised the coconut over his head and began to bash it down on the stick.

'The hardest part,' he said as he worked, 'is getting through the outer husk – all this fibrous stuff. Once you've got that out of the way, you reach the nut on the inside, which you can simply break with a stone.'

By this time there was barely a mark on the coconut, but the stick was reduced to splinters.

'Dang,' was all he said.

However, they both knew that this was a serious situation. They had to find something to drink, soon, or they would be in trouble. The clouds were getting thinner, and the sun for the first time began to show through. It was going to be hot.

'Let's keep looking,' said Frazer. 'Who knows what we'll find.'

At the northern end of their doughnut they saw an encouraging sight – it was the distant outline of an island.

'Do you think there are people there?' asked Amazon excitedly.

'Can't tell. I don't see any smoke from fires . . .'

'How far do you think it is?'

'It's hard to judge. Ten kilometres, maybe?'

'Can we make it there?' Amazon was thinking of the broken canoe – she certainly had no intention of trying to swim through the shark-infested seas.

'You keep asking me stuff I don't know. Maybe . . . But if it's just another uninhabited atoll then we'll have taken the chance for nothing.'

'If only we knew where we were. Wait, your watch. It's got GPS, hasn't it?'

Frazer stared at his wrist. 'Yeah, but that won't really help us without a map. I haven't got the entire longitude and latitude of the globe stored in my head, you know.'

Nevertheless, Frazer flicked through the various buttons on his watch, until he found the GPS function.

'OK, it's working. This is where we're at.'

Frazer held the watch up for Amazon. Its screen read:

18.14.862S
136.12.139W

'What on earth does that mean?'

'Well, these are the latitude and longitude. The first tells that we are 18 degrees, 14 minutes and 862 seconds south of the equator. The second that we are 136 degrees, 12 minutes and 139 seconds west of Greenwich.'

'What use is that?'

'No use at all . . . except, hang on. Yes! I took a reading just before we left the schooner. It should be stored on the watch's memory. Let me see . . . Here it is.'

He showed Amazon the old reading.

18.16.427S
136.21.139W

'I don't quite . . . what does it mean?'

'It means,' said Frazer, 'that the island over there is Uva'avu.'

45

The Rope Trick

They ran back to the broken canoe.

'It doesn't look too bad,' said Frazer. 'But we need to find some way of attaching the outrigger.'

The outrigger section was joined to the main hull by three wooden spars, but each had snapped, leaving just a few strands of shattered wood holding them together.

'Can't we just use the dugout section? I've seen lots of native people do it . . .'

'Fine if you're on a river, but on the open sea you'd roll over and be shark food in no time. No, we've got to fix it.'

'And we can't just wait here until we're rescued?'

As soon as she said it, Amazon knew that that was a forlorn hope. The chances were that every canoe on Uva'avu had been smashed or blown out to sea. And why would they even think of looking here for them? The witnesses – if there were any – to their fate would have seen them being blown in the opposite direction. But there was something else on Frazer's mind.

'They need us. The people over there need help almost as much as we do. Their homes were totally destroyed, and most of their food. My sat phone is the only way of contacting the outside world. And we both know where it is, but nobody else does. We did what we could to help the turtles, now it's time we helped the people. And that includes us!'

'OK, but then how do we fix the canoe?'

'We need some rope to bind those spars together.'

'Where do we get rope from?'

Frazer chewed his lip. 'I've heard about people making rope from hair. I could cut yours off with a sharpened clamshell . . .'

'You are kidding? And your hair's almost as long as mine.'

'Keep your hair on – yes, I was kidding. Maybe we could use strips of bark . . .'

'I saw the women in the village making rope from coconut fibres. They sort of twist and plait them together . . .'

'Yes,' said Frazer in an exasperated tone, 'but we can't even get into the wretched things.'

And then Amazon had a brainwave that might just answer their two pressing needs – for something to drink and for rope.

'How many of those coconut crabs did you see under the trees?' she asked.

'Oh, loads of them. They looked pretty hungry. All the coconuts are in the lagoon, and those crazy crabs don't even know how to sw–'

Frazer looked at Amazon and grinned. 'Clever girl,' he said.

Half an hour later, the cousins had set up a nice little production line. They had retrieved a stash of coconuts from the lagoon, which they had then placed in a line at the edge of the beach. It didn't take long for the hungry crabs to emerge from the undergrowth. Amazon and Frazer watched in fascination as the enormous crustaceans wrestled with the coconuts, shifting them around in their grip until they were satisfied. And then the huge pincers got to work.

Their method was to gouge at the top part of the coconut until they'd made a gash in the green husk, and then tear and scrape away at the fibres until the hard brown kernel was exposed. Then they bore down with all the might of their claws and cracked open the 'lid', with a sound like gunshot.

The first time it happened Frazer stood back while Amazon wrestled the coconut out of the crab's claws. That meant she had the first drink.

'Oh, oh, oh,' was all she could say as she gulped down the milk. 'It is magical.'

She passed it to Frazer, who was trembling with anticipation. The milk was warm, and sweet, and he didn't think he had ever tasted anything finer. He also felt the moisture coursing through his body, bringing back vitality and vigour.

They gave the meat back to the crab and waited for the next crack. It didn't take too long and this time Frazer did the stealing.

Soon they were sated and ready to work on the rope. Now that the crabs had made a start on the coconuts, Frazer was able to use his stick method to prise away most of the husk. Then he and Amazon pulled off the short brown fibres in tussocky clumps of about ten centimetres long.

Then, while Frazer worked at freeing more of the husk, Amazon took over: her fingers were much more adept and nimble than Frazer's. It helped that she had watched the village women at work. She rubbed and twisted the fibres between her hands, binding them together. Then she took another of the clumps and plaited the loose and straggly end together with the first section. It was difficult and painful work – after a while, Amazon's hands were red-raw – but in an hour she had a length of rope as long as her arm.

The second section of rope was ready when Frazer heard a strange noise and looked up.

'What on earth . . . ?'

'Don't disturb me, this is a tricky bit,' said Amazon.

'No, seriously, check this out.'

Amazon tutted and followed Frazer's gaze. She was rewarded with something extraordinary. For there, floating towards their atoll, was a large white box. And draped over the top of it was a human. That it was a living human was indicated by the moaning noises it was emitting.

'Is that . . .?'

'It is.'

The Unexpected Visitor

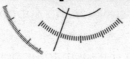

Mr Leopold Chung, Chief Executive of Chung Industries, and the main illegal importer of endangered animals for the pet trade in the United States, was clearly in a very bad way. As they dragged him ashore, he raved and jabbered and flapped weakly at them, and then collapsed on to the sand like a dead Portuguese man-of-war.

There was also a large tear in the seat of his trousers, from which blood was weeping.

Gingerly, Frazer had a look. There was a bite mark, and a chunk of flesh was missing, almost as if a small shark had taken a nibble. And yet it didn't look like a shark bite . . .

'That's nasty,' said Amazon. 'But he's lucky that the sharks didn't follow the blood trail and finish him.'

Chung suddenly opened his eyes wide and screamed, 'Not shark! Huru Huru. He tried to eat me in sea. Began with softest part. It was shark that saved Chung by eating Huru Huru!'

Then he subsided again, and fell back to mumbling and moaning.

Amazon looked at Frazer. 'Is he for real? I mean, did Huru Huru really try to eat him?'

Frazer shrugged. 'Who knows? I think he may have drunk some seawater. It's supposed to make you mad.'

And truly Chung did seem to be deranged.

Amazon held his head while Frazer poured a little of the coconut milk into his parched lips.

He babbled some more and cried out, 'Mummy!' before subsiding again.

'It could just be exposure,' Amazon replied. 'Doesn't really matter, though. We should shove him off on his box again.'

And then Amazon and Frazer both remembered what was in the box. They rushed over to where it lay, washed by the now rather gentle waves. Amazon flicked the catch and opened the lid. Inside, the top layer of little turtles all looked up at her at the same moment. Tears sprang to her eyes and she squeezed Frazer's hand.

'Let's set them free,' said Frazer and they did, gently lifting the turtles down to the water, and watching them swim away. They both knew that many of them would perish before they grew to maturity, but some would make it through, and return, one day, to this beach on this little atoll, to lay their own eggs.

'This is why we do this,' said Frazer. 'For these moments . . .'

'Stupid English. We could have eat those, lived like kings till rescue.'

Amazon and Frazer turned back to the animal trader, who suddenly looked and sounded more like his old self.

'You really are a nasty piece of work,' spat Frazer. 'You were going to leave Bluey to drown back there, and we should have done the same for you.'

'Oh, I know someone come save your friend. No hard feelings. We all on same side now. Humans against the planet. We work together, we win, we live. We make fire, my schooner see it and come save us. I give you lift back to Marquesas. All happy. You help, yes?'

'Chung, you are a joke. I'll tell you what's going to happen. We're going to paddle this canoe back to Uva'avu, radio my dad in the States, who will inform the authorities in Tahiti what's been going on here. What you tried to do with the turtles is against all kinds of international treaties. You'll be rotting in jail for the next ten years.'

Chung tried to curse them in Cantonese, but his throat was too parched. And then his brief moment of lucidity passed, and he relapsed into incoherent mumbling.

Amazon and Frazer dragged him under the shade of a fallen tree and returned to their task. By late afternoon their work was done. They had made three good lengths of rope, and Frazer had first soaked them in seawater, and then used them to bind the broken spars together as best he could.

'They'll tighten as they dry,' he explained, 'and that should help to hold the broken sections together.'

Paddles were a problem. Amazon found a piece of flattened driftwood, hardly bigger than a ping-pong bat, and the best Frazer could do was a stick he found, slightly wider at one end than the other.

'Not great,' said Frazer, looking at what they had, 'but better than nothing.'

It was too late to set off that day, and so they settled down for the night.

Chung was still moaning and jabbering. They left a couple of crab-opened coconuts by his side, and he briefly looked at them and said something, although whether it was to thank them or damn them all to hell they could not know.

'Can we leave him like this?' said Amazon. 'It doesn't seem right. Can't we . . . do something?'

'Well, I'm not sucking the poison out,' replied Frazer. 'Look, the best thing we can do for Chung is to go and get help. That's his only chance. Heck, it's *our* only chance.'

Amazon had to agree.

After what Chung had said about his schooner, they didn't even try to light a fire, although Frazer boasted that his bushcraft skills would have made short work of it. They covered themselves in palm leaves, snuggled down together and, tormented equally by Chung's raving, and by the incessant *no-nos* and mosquitoes, they fell into a fitful sleep.

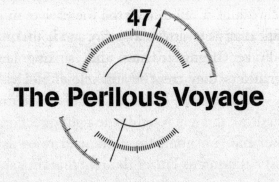

The Perilous Voyage

They woke at first light and checked on Chung. He looked pale and sweaty, and yet was shivering.

Amazon put her hand on his head. 'He's running a fever. That bite must have become infected.'

'They say a human has the dirtiest bite of any animal. Time for us to hit the high seas.'

They pushed the fragile little canoe out into the surf, on the ocean side of the atoll. There was only room for three coconuts, but they were sure that would be plenty for the short voyage. But almost immediately they found a more urgent use for the shells. The canoe, without the raised prow and stern, and lacking the extra planks that were used to build up the sides of the boat, shipped water at an alarming rate. Within five minutes, Amazon and Frazer were sitting in several centimetres of water.

'OK,' said Frazer, 'we take it in turns to bail and paddle. You have the first turn with the coconut.'

So Frazer paddled and Amazon scooped, but it was

a losing battle. Even though the waves were modest, the little craft just wasn't seaworthy, and both Amazon and Frazer began to have that sinking feeling. Nevertheless, they crept steadily closer to Uva'avu. They were helped by favourable winds and currents, which drove them in roughly the right direction.

After half an hour, they changed roles. It was almost a disaster as Frazer thought that they should also change positions. Amazon, trying to crawl round him, set up a crazy wobble, and the canoe rocked from side to side, taking on more seawater with each dip.

Amazon, however, saved the day by jumping over the side and into the sea, and using her hands to steady things. Without her weight, the canoe sat a little higher, and Frazer quickly bailed out the water they'd shipped. He then helped Amazon back on board.

As he did, Amazon noticed his hands: they were scraped raw from the rough paddle he'd been using.

Frazer seemed to notice them for the first time as well. He took off the ragged remains of his T-shirt, tore it into strips and gave two of them to Amazon.

'Wrap these round your hands,' he said, and soon the paddling and bailing began again.

By now the sun was high, and beat down upon them mercilessly. They drained the milk from the second coconut, and then the third, and wished that there had been room on the canoe for more.

But worse things were about to happen than thirst. The coconut-fibre ropes binding the fractured spars of the outrigger just couldn't cope with the sea swell. First the ropes became loose, and the spars buckled at the join. Frazer tried some on-the-go repairs, but it was useless, and soon, one after another, the three spars failed. Without the stability provided by the outrigger, the canoe began to rock viciously, lapping up more water. Amazon's bailing just couldn't keep up. The canoe was soon half full of water. The island was still at least a kilometre away.

But that was not the worst of it. A black fin cut the water away to the right-hand side of the canoe. It sank down again and came up on the right.

'What can we do?' said Amazon desperately.

'Don't worry,' said Frazer bravely, 'that's only a tiddler. It won't bother us. But grab the other paddle. Let's go flat out before she sinks. We might make it.'

They didn't.

Two minutes later, the water was almost up to the gunnels. The shark had disappeared for now, but they knew it would be back.

'We'll have to try to roll her to empty out the water,' said Frazer.

Amazon nodded in reply, but her face was taut with fear. They both slipped into the water, and tried to roll the canoe all the way round. It was much tougher than Frazer had anticipated: eventually they succeeded, but it picked up as much water as it shed.

'We've got to swim for it, Zonnie,' said Frazer.

'I can't . . .' gasped Amazon as she trod water.

'We can do this, cuz,' said Frazer, staring deep into her eyes. 'Try to keep your stroke nice and steady. Thrashing around attracts the . . .'

He didn't want to say the word, and Amazon didn't need to hear it.

'You go first,' he said. 'I'll follow right behind you. Remember, nice steady strokes.'

Amazon was a good swimmer, and, as Frazer recommended, she kept up a rhythmical front crawl. But she hadn't swum much in the open ocean, and she found it much more tiring than doing lengths in the pool. Every so often she would mistime a breath, and take in a mouthful of saltwater.

Of course it didn't help that she was on the very edge of panic. It was fortunate for her that she did not see what Frazer could.

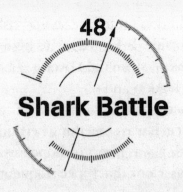

48

Shark Battle

The shark was back.

Frazer, more confident in the water, was also more alert to what was going on around them. He was relieved to see the black tip, meaning it was only a reef shark patrolling the area between the islands, but still, a shark was a shark.

And then, once more, the shark was gone. Frazer, keeping up his own steady freestyle stroke, should have been relieved, but he felt even more uneasy about this sudden disappearance.

He ducked under the water and looked around, ignoring the stinging of the seawater. Nothing. The water was still too thick with sediment stirred up by the storm to allow much visibility.

He swam on more quickly, until he was by Amazon's side. She looked over at him and he smiled. He switched to breaststroke so he could give her a few encouraging words.

'Not far now till we hit the reef. The gap is on the

far side, and I don't think we should risk swimming round the outside. If I'm right, it's high tide and we should be able to swim right over it. Then we cruise through the lagoon and –'

He stopped speaking because of the look on Amazon's face. It was something beyond terror; and mixed in with it was a sort of hopelessness, close to despair. It was a look that spoke eloquently of a huge effort, wasted.

Frazer looked over to his left and saw again a slate-grey fin cutting the water. He knew straight away that this was no black tip. The reef sharks were crafty and careful predators, but also rather timid in the face of a threat. This new arrival was afraid of nothing. And even though Frazer knew it was stupid to ascribe human emotions to animals, he couldn't help but think that this creature bore a grudge. They had taken away its prey once and now it was payback time. Yes, this was the tiger shark, back for revenge.

This was a different situation from the battle over the baby dolphin. There had been no chance to think. The action was too frantic. But now he had a good opportunity to contemplate his and Amazon's fate. Frazer tried to remember everything he'd ever read or heard about defending yourself from a shark attack. Go for the eyes, if you can. Or the nose, which was sensitive. A kick or a punch could sometimes put off an inquisitive shark.

But those things seemed utterly futile against a monster like this. Deep down he knew that Amazon's only hope was if the tiger shark got him first, and that *his* only hope was if it took Amazon.

No! There had to be another way. There was the way of guts. Maybe of sacrifice. Certainly of glory. He was going to attack the shark!

It was ahead of them now, right in between them and the possibility of safety in the lagoon. Frazer looked again at Amazon. She was treading water, and Frazer was incredibly proud of the courage she was showing. But she couldn't stop her teeth from chattering in the cold water.

'Listen to me, Zonnie,' he said, keeping his voice calm. 'I've got a plan. I'm going to swim straight at the tiger. They don't like to be attacked. It has a brain the size of a gumball, and it thinks that anything that attacks it must be a threat. I need you to swim over that way towards the reef. Don't slow down, and don't look back. Just go.'

'NO!' sobbed Amazon. 'I'm not letting you do this. You're a better swimmer than me. You go for it, and I'll . . .'

'Forget it, Zonnie. You're just in my way. Anyway, your parents . . . you've got to find them. Just go, now, or you'll ruin my plan. GO!'

The last 'GO!' was a furious yell. Her heart torn, Amazon began to swim. Then stopped, came back, touched Frazer's face. Their eyes met, in silence, and then she was off again, swimming like she'd never swum before.

Frazer saw the tiger shark still ahead of him, approaching in lazy curves. He kicked out, meaning to rush straight at it. He hoped it would shy away and give them the chance to make it over the reef. It was a slender thread to hang his hopes on.

And now it snapped.

The tiger had sensed the presence of Amazon. Rather than coming for Frazer, it had veered off towards her.

'NOOOOOOO!' he screamed.

He splashed the water, thrashing around, trying to appear like a dying fish to attract the shark. But it wasn't working. The tiger knew what it wanted, and what it wanted was the girl.

Amazon knew nothing of this. She was still swimming for dear life, close now, so close to the reef . . .

49

Payback

The creature dived lower, until her tail almost brushed the soft coral sand on the sea's bottom. And now she saw the shape in the water above her, clearly etched against the light that poured into the ocean from the clear blue sky. This was how she liked to attack, bursting up from underneath.

She beat her tail powerfully and began her attack surge. Somewhere deep in her brain she knew that she had not been seen, and that the attack would succeed. But her mind was also filled with other thoughts. Thoughts of revenge, and what . . .? Something akin to justice. Yes, this was right, so right. Now she was coursing upwards, unstoppable, filled with power and energy.

Closer, closer, closer, and then, with a devastating percussive force that seemed almost not to belong in the animal world, but to the horrors of destruction dreamed up by humankind, she struck.

50

Reunited

Frazer saw it all. The tiger shark surging through the water towards his cousin, and the explosion in the water as, miraculously, wondrously, the dolphin rammed it from below, sending the massive shark

flying a metre up into the air. It was a devastating, indeed almost fatal, blow. The shark could not even swim away, but spiralled down helplessly into the depths.

The mother dolphin leapt through the air once, twice, three times, and then was joined by her baby. In a few powerful strokes Frazer reached Amazon, and they trod the water together as the two dolphins swam and leapt around joyously.

'I can hardly believe it,' said Amazon, 'but she's saying thank you, isn't she, for when we saved the calf . . .'

'I think so,' agreed Frazer, the grin on his face as wide as a giant clam. 'Do you think they'll give us a lift round to the village?'

'It would be nice, wouldn't it? But she's a wild creature, and she's a mother with a baby to look after.'

And, as if to confirm this, the two dolphins suddenly were no longer there, as if they had been merely dreamed up by Amazon and Frazer.

It took them twenty minutes to swim over the reef and reach the land. They hauled themselves up on to the beach, like two exhausted leatherback turtles. It was another half an hour before they made it round the island to the village. They were ragged and filthy and shattered and happy.

The village was once more full of life and activity. The islanders were trying to put their world back together, gathering what they could of their possessions and patching up their ruined homes. Men, women and children were hard at work, foraging and fixing, hammering and hewing. Many of the animals were dead, but one boy was still proudly looking after his puppies, and the occasional dignified pig picked through the rubbish.

Bluey was on the roof of one hut with Matahi and Oti, weaving new palm leaves into the thatch, when Amazon and Frazer entered the village. Matahi had used a hatchet to cut the chain between the handcuffs, but the steel rings were still around Bluey's wrists. Amazon could tell from his face that he had spent a long, dark night, his soul racked with horror and regret over the loss of the two young Trackers, whose care had been in his hands.

Frazer called out, 'Hey, Bluey, nice bracelets. You got a matching necklace and earrings?'

Bluey looked up from his work. His face registered, in quick succession, puzzlement, disbelief, astonishment and joy. And then, entirely disregarding every health and safety rule he had ever been taught, he jumped straight down from the roof, to land at the feet of Amazon and Frazer.

The three Trackers hugged, while the villagers gathered round, chattering excitedly, and grinning with joy at the return of the lost children.

'I thought you guys were dead. Stone dead. Like, as dead as you could be.'

'If it hadn't been for a dolphin, we would have been,' said Amazon. 'And Frazer was pretty cool, as well. For a Yank.'

Frazer smiled. 'Hey, you Brits did OK too. And we both bailed out the Aussies! And, guess what, we saved the baby turtles, so we can chalk this up as mission accomplished! But it's a long story. So what's been happening here?'

'Well, no one was killed, but you can see the mess the storm made. The people here are pretty resilient, but they need help, and there's no way to get word out.'

'My village will recover,' said Matahi proudly. 'My people are brave and strong. But yes, we will need help to rebuild . . .'

'I think I can lend a hand there,' said Frazer.

Bluey gave him a quizzical look. Frazer pointed to the tree, still sprouting the sat phone fruit, safe above the flood.

'I'll call my dad. He'll pull some strings. He'll want to know about the turtles. I guess it won't be long before a boat comes with supplies for the island, and a lift out of here for us.'

'But you will come back?' asked Oti quietly. Or perhaps, rather than a question, it was a statement.

'Yes,' said Amazon and squeezed his hand, which sent the boy off on a series of cartwheels that managed both to express his joy and hide his embarrassment.

Matahi smiled.

'And we will hear your story. You must tell it well so that we can see the pictures in our minds. But first I think that we may be able to gather together enough for a feast. A small feast . . .'

Without the jamming of the signal, it took no more than a few seconds for Frazer to get through to Hal Hunt. Hal's gruff voice was not mellowed by the distorting effect of the satellite.

'What the heck took you so long to call me?' he barked. 'And how are those turtles? Or were you too busy working on your tan to notice?'

'Turtles are good, Dad. And sorry about not calling. I guess we had a few . . . problems. There was an attack by killer squid, a shark issue, a typhoon, a castaway interlude, another shark issue and a couple of bad guys who wanted to bump us off. You know, the usual TRACKS stuff. So we were kinda busy. But, yeah, we saved a whole bunch of baby turtles.'

And then Frazer saw the yearning look on Amazon's face, and took advantage of the stunned silence on the other end of the phone to add, 'Dad, I'm going to hand you over to Amazon now. I think she needs to . . . well, you know.'

'Hi, Uncle Hal,' Amazon said, frail hope and deep yearning mixing together in her voice. 'Have you . . .?'

'It's good to hear your voice, Amazon.' The gruffness had gone from Hal's voice, replaced by an unaccustomed tenderness.

'But my parents . . . I need to know.'

A pause.

'I'm sorry, Amazon, but there's still nothing. We've been following up various reports of light aircraft in the area, checking possible flight paths . . . Really, Amazon, we're doing everything we can.'

'I need to be there too.'

'I know you do, honey. I'm arranging for a ship to come and pick you up. You'll be back here in a few days. Use the time well. Teach the island people about turtle conservation. Pass on your skills. It's the only way ahead . . . for all of you.'

'We will, Uncle Hal.'

Suddenly Hal Hunt's voice changed again.

'Hey, can I speak to my old friend Omo – or rather Tuvali as he calls himself these days. It's been a long time since we had a chinwag.'

'Oh, Uncle Hal, I've got some sad news for you . . .'

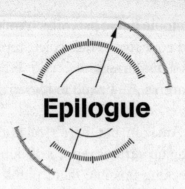

Epilogue

The relief ship from Tahiti was three days away, and so, paddling a big canoe salvaged by the villagers from the treetop in which it had been deposited by the storm, Amazon, Frazer, Bluey, Matahi and Oti set off to pick up Leopold Chung from the neighbouring island.

However, on reaching the atoll, there was no sign of the man, other than a pile of empty coconut shells.

'What do you think happened to him?' asked Amazon.

'Well,' said Frazer, 'either he really was mad and swam for it, which means right now he's working his way through the digestive system of that tiger shark, or maybe the *Tian-long* came and picked him up. My guess is that we haven't seen the last of that crook.'

On their way back to Uva'avu, they were joined, briefly, by a dolphin and her calf. They may have been paying their respects. Or perhaps they were merely chasing the flying fish, which sailed over the canoe.

'Anyone for fish baseball?' said Frazer, which earned him one of Amazon's friendlier punches.

TOP 10 FACTS:
SHARKS

1. **SHARKS**' 'bones' aren't actually made of bone! Their skeletons are formed from cartilage. If you want to know what cartilage is like, feel your ear – it's made from cartilage too.

2. The teeth of a **SHARK** grow in long rows. As the teeth are ground down or fall out, new ones from the other rows come forward to fill the slot – like a conveyor belt. This continues for their entire lives.

3. **SHARKS'** eyes are on the sides of their heads, so they can see nearly 360 degrees. Their panoramic view of the undersea world only has two 'blind spots', one in front of the snout and the other directly behind the head.

4. **SHARKS** need to move oxygen-rich water over their gills constantly in order to breathe, and mostly this means continually swimming. If they stopped, they would 'drown'!

5. The **TIGER SHARK** will eat whenever an opportunity presents itself or swims by! It will eat other sharks, turtles, whales, dolphins, fish and squid. But stranger things have been found in their stomachs, including car tyres and number plates!

6. While the **TIGER SHARK** is considered to be one of the most dangerous sharks for humans, second after the great white, the number of attacks is low. More people are killed by bee stings than by sharks.

7. Although we are not in much danger from **SHARKS**, they are threatened by us. Forty million are killed every year just for their fins, which are made into soup. The rest of the animal is thrown away.

8. Around 21 species of **SHARK** live off the British coast. The biggest is the **BASKING SHARK**, which eats plankton and grows up to 11 metres. Shark attacks in European waters are extremely rare. Since 1847, there have only been two unprovoked shark attacks in England, neither of which proved fatal.

9. **SHARKS** have been around for about 400 million years, even before dinosaurs roamed the earth!

10. Like humans, **SHARKS** are at the top of the food chain. Just as humans rule the land, sharks rule the sea!

TOP 10 FACTS: LEATHERBACK TURTLES

1. There are seven living species of sea turtle: the **FLATBACK SEA TURTLE**, the **GREEN SEA TURTLE**, the **HAWKSBILL**, **KEMP'S RIDLEY SEA TURTLE**, the **LOGGERHEAD SEA TURTLE**, the **OLIVE RIDLEY SEA TURTLE** and the **LEATHERBACK SEA TURTLE**.

2. The **LEATHERBACK TURTLE** is the largest of all living turtles.

3. **LEATHERBACK TURTLES** usually weigh 250–700 kg, but the largest ever recorded weighed 916 kg and was found on a beach in Wales.

4. Despite their size, **LEATHERBACK TURTLES** are the fastest moving reptiles in the water. The quickest leatherback turtle ever recorded swam at 21.92 mph.

5. **LEATHERBACK TURTLES** don't have teeth. Instead, they have sharp, snapping beaks with backwards spines on their upper lips, which help them swallow food.

6. The upper side of **LEATHERBACK TURTLES** is dark grey and black, but their underside is light in colour.

7. **LEATHERBACKS** live from the far north of Alaska to the southernmost tip of New Zealand, in the Pacific, Atlantic and Indian Oceans.

8. Jellyfish are the favourite food of **LEATHERBACK TURTLES**. They also eat squid, and other small sea creatures.

9. Despite their wide distribution, **LEATHERBACK TURTLES** are facing extinction. In 1982 there were estimated to be 115,000 adult females. By 1996 this had fallen to 30–40,000. In the Pacific Ocean today, where the action of *Shark Adventure* takes place, as few as 2,300 adult females now remain.

10. The main threats to **LEATHERBACK TURTLES** are loss of habitat, climate change and poaching of their eggs. Local communities are being taught how to protect the turtles' nesting beaches, and an initiative to save Pacific leatherbacks has begun in Costa Rica.